"Good morning."

She looked up, and for a second her heart stopped.

And then he moved, stepped forward into the room, and as the light hit his face Annie felt the stupid, foolish hope drain away and her heart started again.

Crazy. For a moment there—but it was silly. It was just because she'd been thinking about him—

"You okay?" he asked, his voice low and rough and strangely sensuous. "You look as if you've seen a ghost."

She nearly laughed aloud, and dragged her eyes from the battered, lived-in face in front of her, staring down in bewilderment at her shaking hands. Lord, she should have stopped doing this after all these years, clutching at straws, seeing him in any random stranger, but there was just something—

"Sorry. You reminded me of someone."

A BRIDE WORTH WAITING FOR

Caroline Anderson

Heart *to* Heart

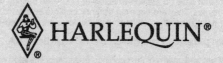

TORONTO • NEW YORK • LONDON
AMSTERDAM • PARIS • SYDNEY • HAMBURG
STOCKHOLM • ATHENS • TOKYO • MILAN • MADRID
PRAGUE • WARSAW • BUDAPEST • AUCKLAND

ISBN 0-373-03877-1

A BRIDE WORTH WAITING FOR

First North American Publication 2006.

Caroline Anderson has the mind of a butterfly. She's been a nurse, a secretary, a teacher, run her own soft-furnishing business and now she's settled on writing. She says, "I was looking for that elusive something. I finally realized it was variety, and now I have it in abundance. Every book brings new horizons and new friends, and in between books I have learned to be a juggler. My teacher husband, John, and I have two beautiful and talented daughters, Sarah and Hannah, umpteen pets and several acres of Suffolk that nature tries to reclaim every time we turn our backs!"

Join Caroline Anderson on a wonderful
romantic escape. Her stories are
emotional and touching.

Books by Caroline Anderson

HARLEQUIN ROMANCE®
3806—THE PREGNANT TYCOON
3826—THE PREGNANCY SURPRISE

PROLOGUE

'IT'S over.'

For a moment he didn't move, just stood there and let it sink in. Then he turned slowly round and scanned her face.

'They've got him?'

Ruth nodded. 'They caught up with him in a villa just outside Antibes. He'd got sloppy—maybe he thought we'd given up.'

He grunted. 'Fat chance after what that bastard's done. So he's finally going to be put away—well, I hope they throw the book at him. They will if I have anything to do with it. Never mind the other things he's done and the countless lives he's ruined, that animal owes me nine years.'

Ruth—his researcher and friend, his ex-colleague and the woman who'd kept him sane for all that time—shook her head. 'Sorry, Michael. He's dead.'

He swore quietly and succinctly and with considerable feeling. 'What happened?'

'There was a girl there with him. Frank didn't say what he'd done to her, but I'm sure we can fill in the details. She shot him after they stormed the house—they were cuffing him, and she just shot him through the head with his own gun at point-blank range. Said he deserved it.'

'Is that the official version?'

Ruth shook her head and smiled. 'Oh, no. I gather his gun went off in the confusion. Conveniently.'

He nodded, glad the girl wouldn't be punished for what amounted to a public service. 'Good for her,' he said softly.

'I would have liked ten minutes alone with him, though, before she did it.'

'Absolutely. You and all the others. It was too good for him, but whatever. It's over—that's all that matters really.'

It was. And that meant they'd all be safe—him, Ruth, Annie and the son he had yet to get to know. The threat hanging over them was gone, finally, after all these years.

And now it was time for the last act.

He felt the rush of adrenaline, the nerves, the anticipation—like the start of an operation, but worse, because he was personally involved in this one. It wasn't something he could remain detached about. No way.

'What about the others?' he asked, his voice rough—rougher even than usual, rusty with emotion and lack of use.

'They were picking them up when Frank rang me. They've been closing in for days, had everyone under surveillance. They did a dawn swoop. It's massive. It'll be on the news.'

'So it's official?'

Ruth nodded. 'Yes—just about. I expect someone will come and see you. Frank rang me this morning—I'm surprised he hasn't called you.'

'He may have done. The phone rang when I was in the shower. I ignored it. I'll call him now.'

And then he could get things in motion. He'd been on ice for eight, nearly nine years, and now the waiting was over.

'Fancy living here?' he asked quietly. 'Swapping houses? Just for a while. I could use the flat as an excuse to be there.'

There was a silence, and as it stretched out he turned and studied her thoughtfully.

'Am I missing something?' he asked, and she gave a wry little smile.

'If you don't need me, there's somewhere else I'd rather be.'

'Tim?'

She nodded. 'He's asked me to marry him—again. And somehow, with this finally over, I feel free at last—as if the debt's paid and I can move on. And I do love him.'

He closed his eyes, let out his breath on a short huff of laughter before the emotion choked him. 'Ruth—that's great. Wonderful. I'm really glad for you. It's about time—and of course I don't need you. Not that much—not enough to get in the way of this. You know I'd never stand in your way. I've asked too much from you for too long as it is—'

'No. It's been fine. I needed your support every bit as much as you needed mine. You kept me safe, gave me a reason to live when it all fell apart, and I'll be eternally grateful for that, but...'

'But you don't need me any more,' he prompted.

'Not now.' She smiled gently at him. 'I'll always need your friendship, and you'll always have mine. You know that. But Tim's there for me now. I need to be with him.'

'How much does he know?'

She shrugged. 'Enough. I never thought I could ever trust a man again after what happened. And I certainly never thought I'd love again after David died. But—with Tim, it's all fallen into place, and I feel I can start again. Draw a line under this, get on with my life.'

'I'm so glad for you,' he said softly.

'Thank you. I'll still work for you,' she added. 'If you want me to.'

His grin was crooked. 'I don't know. This changes things, doesn't it? I don't need to write for a living. Not any more. I might try something different. Grow grapes or something. We'll talk about it. Why don't you have a holiday—six months? I'll take a break from my writing. That should give us both time to sort out the future.'

'Sounds perfect.'

'I'll still pay you, of course, in the meantime. Put you on a retainer or something—and don't argue.'

She opened her mouth, shut it again and smiled. 'So when do you want me to move out—if you still do?'

He felt the lick of adrenaline in his veins. 'Please—if you feel you can. I can use the excuse of refurbishing the building—that should give me plenty of opportunities to talk to her. How soon could you move?'

'The weekend? I don't know—the sooner the better, really. I can't imagine not being with Tim now. I'll talk to him when I see him.'

'You seeing him today?'

Ruth nodded. 'I'll go back at lunchtime—he's off today.'

'Go now. I've got things to do as well—people to talk to. We'll meet up again later in the week.'

She nodded again, then hugged him, the unprecedented physical contact taking him by surprise. In nine years he'd always kept his distance, giving her space, careful to preserve her comfort zone because of what had happened to her. Now it seemed she didn't need it any more.

'I hope it works out for you with Annie and Stephen,' she said a little unevenly. 'You deserve to be happy. It's been far, far too long—for all of us.'

And for ever for David. He put away that thought, shaking his head slightly to clear it. It was time for the living, now. Time to move on.

Time for the last and maybe most important op of his life. He'd planned it meticulously over the past year, and thrown out each plan. He was going to have to fly this one by the seat of his pants, but he was going to succeed. He had to. The stakes were too high for him to fail.

'You take care, babe. Tell Tim from me he's a lucky man.'

He watched Ruth go, then sat down, staring blindly out over the gently rolling fields. He could see a tractor working in the distance, the gulls wheeling in its wake, dots against the vivid blue of the sky.

It was still warm during the day, even though it was September. It reminded him of France. That late September had been just like this, with glorious sunny days and then later, moving into October, clear, starry nights when the temperature would fall and their breath would fog on the cold night air as they walked hand in hand between the vines.

He shut his eyes, seeing her again, young and vibrant and full of laughter, her eyes bubbling over with joy. She'd tasted so sweet, so eager and passionate—so utterly irresistible. He hadn't been able to resist—not that night, knowing things were coming to a head. He'd lost himself in her, and she'd given him everything. Her ring. Her heart.

And a son who didn't know him.

Yet.

His fingers closed over the ring. He'd worn it on a chain around his neck for so many years now the chain had worn a groove in the band. She'd given it to him that night to keep him safe, after they'd made love, and he'd treasured it all this time. It was almost as if he'd survive as long as he had it on him. He'd never taken it off, but he would now. He'd have to, or she'd see it and know, before he was ready.

He took it off, slipped it into his wallet, fingering the lump it made in the soft leather.

Maybe soon he could tell her the truth. Not yet, though.

First, she had to get to know him again, get to know the real man, the man he was now. And he had to get to know her.

At least they were free now—him free to woo her, her free to love him if she would. That was by no means certain, but he wouldn't allow the thought of failure. Not now, not at this stage.

He moved away from the window, his eyes no longer focusing on the tractor in the distance, but on his reflection in the mirror. Dispassionately, with clinical detachment, he studied the man who stared back at him.

Would he get away with it?

He didn't look like the man Annie had fallen in love with. Time and the surgery that had saved his life had seen to that. The results were passable—battered, but passable. He wasn't actively ugly, at least; he should be grateful for that. He wondered if his own parents would have recognised him. At least they'd been spared seeing him at his worst. It would have killed his mother. It had damn nearly killed him.

He turned away, reached for the phone, dialled a long-familiar number.

'It's me,' he said economically.

He could almost hear the smile at the other end.

'Michael. Welcome back to the real world.'

CHAPTER ONE

'HIYA.'

Annie was just about to close when she heard Ruth's voice behind her. 'Hiya yourself, stranger,' she said, turning with a grin. 'I missed you over the weekend. How are you?'

'Better than you, apparently. You look tired, Annie.'

She flapped her hand. 'I'm always tired. I've been tired for years,' she said, dismissing it. 'Don't worry about me, I'm used to it. What can I get you? Coffee? Tea?'

'Nothing. I don't want to stop you, you're about to close.'

'I have done,' she said, shutting the door and flipping the sign in the window. 'There's half a pot of coffee left and it's only going down the drain if we don't drink it. Want to share it with me?'

'If you're sure you've got time. What about Stephen?'

'He's got chess club.' She reached for the cups. 'So, how are you? I haven't seen you for days.' Annie scanned Ruth's face, checking out the slightly heightened colour in her cheeks, the sparkle in her eyes, as if something was bottled up inside her and threatening to spill over. She'd be a lousy poker player, she thought with a grin.

'OK, come on, spit it out. What's going on? Where have you been?'

Ruth gave a self-conscious chuckle. 'At Tim's. Actually, I've got something to tell you.'

'I'd never have guessed!' Annie teased, plonking the full cups on the round table by the window and pulling up a chair. 'Come on, then—tell away.'

Ruth laughed softly and sat, making a production of opening the creamer and tipping it into the cup, stirring it unnecessarily long until Annie was ready to scream.

'Ruth?' she prompted.

'Sorry.' Her smile was—good heavens—shy? 'I'm getting married.'

Annie's heart squeezed tight, and she leant over and hugged Ruth, pressing her eyes firmly shut to hold back the unexpected prickle of tears. 'Ruth, that's fantastic!' she said, her voice choked. 'When did he ask you? I take it we're talking about your gorgeous policeman, since you spent the weekend with him?'

Ruth sniffed and sat back, her cheeks pink. 'Of course it's Tim. And he's asked me over and over again. I said yes this morning. I'm going to move in with him.'

'Well, of course you will.' She listened to herself in dismay. Did she really sound so bereft? How silly. She injected a little enthusiasm and interest into her voice. 'Will you be far away? Where does he live?'

'Not far. Only three miles. He's been asking me endlessly to move in with him, dropping hints for ages before he began proposing—and I've finally decided to do it.'

'Oh, Ruth, I'm so pleased for you! I wondered what was going on—you've been looking so much happier since you met him.'

'I have been. I am.'

'It shows.' Annie smiled wistfully. 'Lucky old you. You know, I did wonder at one point, when there didn't seem to be a man in your life at all, if you'd got some kind of thing going on with Michael—'

'Michael? Good grief, no!' She laughed and shook her head. 'Hardly.'

'Is he so bad?'

Ruth chuckled. 'No, he's not bad at all. Far from it. I

suppose if he was your type, you'd think he was very sexy in a rather brooding sort of way. I don't know. You can judge for yourself on Monday.'

'Monday?'

'Mmm. He's coming over then—I'm moving out at the weekend, and he's going to start tearing the place apart. He's jumped at the chance to get in there. He wants to refurbish the whole building, in fact; says it's long overdue, which it is.'

Annie blinked in surprise. 'Does he have time?'

Ruth nodded. 'He's going to have a break from writing, and he's told me to take a holiday, so I am. I think he's planning a little physical work to free up his thoughts and, let's face it, the place could do with a hefty dose of TLC. I think he's looking forward to pushing his sleeves up and getting stuck in.'

Her heart thudded unexpectedly. 'Wow. So I get to meet the great man at last.'

She chewed her lip absently. She'd never met her landlord, not in the seven years since he'd bought the Ancient House. Ruth had been the go-between, working for him as his researcher and living here in the flat that occupied the whole of the top floor, but curiously Michael himself had never darkened her door, so she knew little about him except that he was a writer—a hugely successful one, if the best seller lists were to be believed.

That was probably why she'd never met him. Too busy and important to trouble himself with some trifling investment property—or so she'd thought. He certainly didn't need her contribution to his income if the rumours of his advances were true.

Roger had loved his books—he'd even met him once, but she'd been out when he called and so she'd missed him, to her disappointment. But he hadn't described him as broodingly sexy—

'I wonder if he'll use the refurb as an excuse to put my rent up?' she murmured, dragging herself back to practical matters and the here and now.

Ruth shrugged. 'Dunno. I doubt it. You'll have to ask him.' She pulled a face. 'It'll be odd not living here after so long.'

'Seven years. It'll be weird without you. I'll miss you.' Unaccountably she felt herself tearing up again and looked away crossly. 'Sorry, I'm being an idiot. I'm delighted for you, I really am. It's just—'

'You'll miss me. I know. I'll miss you, too.' Ruth patted her arm awkwardly. 'You'll be fine. You've got my mobile number—perhaps we could go out for a drink one evening, if Stephen's with a friend or something?'

'That would be lovely,' she said, knowing quite well it was unlikely to happen but grateful to Ruth for suggesting it. 'Thank you for all you've done for me in the past few years, especially since Roger died. You've been a star.'

'My pleasure. You've been a good friend to me, too, Annie. There were times when I couldn't have got through without you.'

That unexpected frankness was nearly her undoing. Annie swallowed and gave a little shrug. 'What are friends for? I'm glad you've found someone. You deserve to be happy.'

Ruth nodded and turned her attention to her coffee, looking at it rather than at Annie, stirring it with meticulous care. 'I just wish you could be as happy,' she said quietly after a moment. 'I know you and Roger were very fond of each other, but you weren't exactly soul mates, were you? You've never really told me about Stephen's father, but I get the feeling you're still a little in love with him. Is there any chance—?'

Annie felt her smile slip. 'No. He's dead—years ago, before I started running this place. The way I felt—well, it was a one-off, crazy thing. I don't know if it was the real thing, but it certainly felt like it at the time. He was French, and such a charmer—I just fell for that broken English and gorgeous, sexy accent hook, line and sinker. I adored him, but you can't base a marriage on it. At least we didn't have time to get bored with each other. I don't know. It might have worked given time, who knows, but I doubt it. We just didn't get the chance to find out.'

'But maybe now—if the right man came along—?'

She shook her head. 'No. I don't need any more heart-ache, and nor does Stephen. He's lost two fathers, although he only ever knew Roger. I think that's enough for anyone.'

Ruth was quiet for a moment, then she looked up and searched Annie's face. 'Do you think Stephen's suffered for not knowing his real father?'

Annie shook her head slowly. 'No—not really. I know we had an unconventional marriage, but Roger was a good father to all the children. Stephen adored him, and I would have been horribly lost without him—even if I could never compete with his first wife.'

'Ah, yes. The amazing Liz. Ghosts are always the hard-est. She was a bit of a legend, by all accounts. They still talk about her, you know.'

Annie nodded. 'She was certainly loved in the village. Her death was an awful shock to everyone. I couldn't be-lieve it. She'd been my college lecturer, you know—taught me everything I knew about catering, but she was more than that, even then. She was a friend, a real friend, and I was lost when she died, but at least we'd set this place up by then, so she saw her dream become reality. Still. Time moves on, and they're together again now. And you've got your Tim. I really, really hope you're happy together.'

'We will be. Do keep in touch. Can I come and have coffee still?'

Annie laughed. 'Of course. I run a coffee shop—what else would you do?'

'But you're busy.'

'Never too busy for a friend. Please come. Don't be a stranger. I couldn't bear to lose you, too.'

'You won't lose me—promise.'

Ruth hugged her again, and then went out, running up the stairs to the flat above to start her packing, and Annie scrubbed the kitchen until it sparkled, determined not to let the stupid tears fall. It wasn't as if Ruth was a bosom buddy, but as busy as she was, Ruth was probably one of her closest friends. Bringing up the children and working the hours she did didn't leave a lot of time for socialising.

She straightened up, threw the tea towel she'd used for polishing the worktops into a bag to take home, and looked round, checking to make sure she was ready for the morning.

What would her landlord make of it, she wondered? And how would he want to change it? Refurb covered a multitude of sins. A shiver of apprehension went down her spine. The Ancient House was Grade II listed, so there were restrictions on what he could do to it—she hoped. She didn't want it to change. She'd had enough change recently. But what if he wanted to throw her out and turn it back into a house? That was always a possibility now she was the only tenant.

It was old, very old, a typical low Tudor house, stretching all across one side of the square, with a big heavy door in the centre that led to a small rectangular entrance hall. There was a door straight ahead that led to the flat above, another door leading to Miller's, her little tearoom that ran front to back on the right of the door, and one opening into the left-hand end that was occupied by the little antique shop.

Ex-antique shop, she reminded herself, now that Mary had wound down her business and closed the door finally for the last time only a week ago, so what better time for him to move in and make changes?

More changes. Heavens, her life was full of them recently. Roger's death in June last year had been the first. Even though they'd been waiting for it, it had still been a shock when it came. Still, they'd got through somehow, comforting each other, and it hadn't been all bad.

Kate, Roger's younger daughter, had got the grades she needed for uni, and there had been tears, of course, because her father hadn't been there to see her success. And Annie, telling her how proud he would have been, had reduced them all to tears again.

In September the girls had gone away—Vicky, the eldest, back to Leicester for her second year and Kate to Nottingham to start her degree, and the house had seemed unnaturally silent and empty. Stephen was back at school, and without the tearoom Annie would have gone crazy.

She'd grown used to the silence, though, and the holidays since had seemed almost too noisy. Much as she loved them, she'd been glad this September when the girls had gone away again and taken their chaos and untidiness with them, but without them, and with Ruth moving on, it would be very quiet. Probably too quiet.

She laughed softly to herself.

'You are perverse. One minute it's too noisy, the next it's too quiet. Nothing's ever right.'

Still, from Monday things would liven up with the refurb

starting. And she'd finally get to meet her landlord, the broodingly sexy Michael Harding. Whatever that implied.

Well, she hoped it turned out right and he didn't have an ulterior motive. Here she was trying to work out what broodingly sexy might mean, when all the time he might be going to give her notice or put up her rent. It wouldn't be unreasonable if he did, but it would be the last straw.

Roger's pension kept the girls in uni. The tearoom provided the means to keep her and Stephen and run the house, but the balance was fine and she didn't need anything unexpected thrown into the equation.

There was always the trust fund, but she had no intention of touching that, even if she could. It was Stephen's, from some unknown distant cousin who'd died intestate; it had been passed down to him as the man's youngest living relative, which was apparently how the law worked. She wasn't going to argue, and as only one of the trustees she wasn't sure she could get access to it, even to provide for her son. Still, to know it was there was like a safety net, carefully invested for the future.

Whatever that might hold. Maybe Monday would bring some answers.

She went home, cutting the corner to where their pretty Georgian house stood at right angles to the tearoom, centred on the left hand side of the square. Like the Ancient House, Beech House occupied a prominent position in the centre of the village, its elegant, symmetrical façade set back behind a low wall enclosing the pretty front garden.

The fact that it was so lovely hardly ever registered with Annie, though. For her, the main feature was its convenience. It was handy being so close. That was why Liz had chosen to open the tearoom there, of course, and its proximity had been a godsend while the children were young.

It didn't feel like home, though. It never really had. She

was like a caretaker, and with Roger gone and the girls flying the nest she wondered what on earth she was going to do with it. Keep it for ever, so the girls felt they could always come home? Or just until Stephen was eighteen?

Another nine years. Heavens. The thought of another nine years of this was enough to send her over the brink.

She closed the door behind her, leant back on it and listened to the silence. She was right, it was too quiet, and Stephen with his bubbly chatter wouldn't be home until eight. God, the house was so *empty*.

She made herself a cup of tea, then settled down on the sofa in the little sitting room to watch the news for company. She kicked off her shoes, tucked her feet under her bottom and flicked on the TV with the remote control.

And then she froze, riveted by the commentary and the picture she saw unfolding before her eyes.

'—a vineyard in the Rhône valley, high up on the steeply terraced hillside where only the most exclusive wines can justify the exorbitant labour costs for handpicking the grapes—unless, like Claude Gaultier, you use a migrant workforce.'

The reporter waved an arm behind him at the serried ranks of vines, bursting with fruit just starting to ripen. 'For the past eleven years, the vines here have been worked by what amounts to slave labour, the workers kept in very basic accommodation and forced to work hugely long hours in appalling conditions on these steep mountainsides to bolster Gaultier's extortionate profit.'

The picture scanned over the familiar scenery, the bunkhouse, the farmhouse where she'd cooked, the winery, the terraces where they'd walked hand in hand—

'All the workers were young men, most of whose parents had paid extraordinary sums to give them an opportunity to escape from countries such as Albania to the riches of

Western Europe. They were lied to, cheated for the sake of money, but at least these young men were only forced to work hard. The young women, on the other hand, were shipped all over Europe and sold into prostitution, many of them in London and Manchester, and the fate of these innocent girls has been far worse. The dawn raid today, the culmination of a decade of work by the security services of several countries, has seen many of Gaultier's accomplices arrested. Gaultier himself, the mastermind behind this hideous empire trafficking in innocent lives, died resisting arrest when his house in Antibes was stormed this morning, and it must be said there will be few tears shed for this most evil and wanted of men.'

The picture returned to the newsroom, and Annie stared blankly at the screen.

Dear God. She'd always known the conditions there were dreadful, but she'd had no idea they were that bad. People-trafficking? Slave labour? She'd not really been involved with the labour force, more with the managers. Like Etienne. And Etienne had taken her mind off anything but him, from the moment she'd set eyes on him...

'Bonjour.'

She looked up, her heart hitching into her throat at the slow, lazy lilt of his voice. Blue eyes, a smile that started gradually and kicked up both corners of his mouth to reveal perfect, even teeth—no. Not perfect. Not quite. One of them was chipped, and his nose was nothing to write home about, but the smouldering eyes and the lazy smile were enough to counteract that in spades.

'Bonjour,' she replied, her hand hovering over a steaming dish of lamb casserole. *'Desirez-vous un peu de ragout?'*

The smile widened. *'Tu,'* he murmured. *'Vous* is too—how you say—formal?—for me.'

She felt herself colouring. 'Oh. Sorry. I thought it was correct.'

He grinned. 'It is—but we do not need to be correct, *hein*, you and me?'

She found herself smiling back, her heart fluttering against her ribs like a thing demented. Her hand still hovered over the casserole, her eyes trapped by his. 'How did you know I was English?' she said breathlessly.

'Your delightful accent,' he replied, in a delightful accent of his own, and her heart melted into a puddle at his feet. He held out his hand. 'Etienne Duprés—at your service, *mademoiselle.'*

'Annie Shaw,' she said breathlessly, and he took her hand, wrapping it in warm, hard fingers. His thumb slid over the back of it, grazing it gently, sending shivers up her spine while his eyes locked with hers.

'Enchanté, mademoiselle,' he murmured, then after an age he bent to press his lips to her hand—but not the back. Oh, no. He turned it over and pressed his lips firmly and devastatingly to the palm, then folded her fingers over to enclose the kiss and straightened up to meet her eyes again, a slow, sexy grin teasing at his mouth.

He wasn't the only one who was enchanted. Annie could hardly think straight for the rest of the meal, dishing up for the family and the skilled staff. The grape-pickers had their own catering arrangements in the bunkhouse, and her job was to help Madame Chevallier to cook for the permanent staff who ran the vineyard. And if she didn't want to lose her job, she'd better concentrate on what she was doing.

Finally they were all served and seated, and she took her own meal and went and sat in the only space left. Which just happened, by a curious coincidence, to be next to Etienne Duprés.

'You must be new here; I haven't seen you,' she said, but he shook his head.

'I have been away—*en vacances*. On holiday?'

She nodded. 'I wondered.'

'So you have been thinking about me. *Bon*,' he said with satisfaction. 'And you must be new here.'

She nodded again. 'I'm here for the harvest. I'm sorry, my French is dreadful—'

He waved a hand dismissively. 'I'm sure we understand what is necessary,' he said, and his eyes locked with hers again, their message unmistakeable.

'You're outrageous,' she told him, blushing, and he laughed, not a discreet chuckle but the real thing, throwing back his head and letting out a deep rumble of a belly-laugh that had all the others smiling and nodding and ribbing him.

'No, *mademoiselle*, I only tell the truth.'

And he was right, of course. She could understand enough of the muddle of his French and English to know precisely what he was trying to say to her, and he seemed to be able to understand English better than he could speak it, so between them they managed.

After all, it didn't take much facility with the language to walk side by side along the rows of vines in the setting sun, and to pause under the spreading branches of an old oak tree and exchange slow, lingering kisses.

That was all they ever did, and then he'd sigh and turn back to the path and wrap his arm around her, tucking her into his side and shortening his stride to hers as they strolled back to the farmhouse. On her nights off he took her to the village and they sat in the bar and talked in their halting French and English until late, then he walked her home, pausing to kiss her under the tree.

She learned that he was an estate manager, that he'd trained in Australia and California, that he had been brought in to supervise the production of the exclusive and very expensive wine produced here. She told him she had trained as a cook, but was going to run a tearoom—a café—called Miller's, with a friend in a village in Suffolk on her return.

He seemed interested, so she told him about Liz Miller, and about their plans and how Liz was getting it off the ground now and how they'd share it when she got home, and he grinned and promised to come and visit her. 'To take tea—in Miller's, a very English tearoom. I shall look forward to this. After the harvest,' he promised, and she believed him.

She learned to tease him, and he teased her back. One evening as they sat in the bar she reached out a hand and ran her fingertip down the bumpy and twisted length of his nose. 'What happened to it?' she asked, and he laughed.

'I was—*pouf*!' he said, making a fist and holding it to his nose and grinning.

'You had a fight?'

He nodded, blue eyes laughing.

'Don't tell me—over a woman?'

The grin widened. '*Mais oui!* What else is there to fight about?'

She chuckled. 'And did you win?'

'*Bien sûr!* Of course. I always win the lady.'

'And was she married, this lady?' she asked, suddenly needing the answer to be no, and he frowned, serious for once.

'*Non.* Of course not. I would not do that. I am—how do you say it? A gentleman.'

And he was. He walked her home, kissed her lingeringly, sighed and handed her in through the door like the gentleman he said he was, then wandered off, whistling softly under his breath.

A week later, one cold October night, he seemed different. Distracted, somehow, and for once not focusing on her with that strange intensity, as if she was the centre of his world. At least not then, not in the bar, but later on the way home he drew her off the path, away from the farm buildings and up into a little wood, then he turned her into his arms and kissed her in a way he'd never kissed her before.

His body was strong and lean and full of coiled energy, warm and hard under her hands, his heart pounding against her chest, a strange urgency about him. He'd always been playful before, but that night there was no time for play. He kissed her as if he'd die without her, touched her as if she was the most precious thing in the universe. They made love then for the first and last time, on a bed of fallen leaves under the stars, and in his arms she found a happiness she'd never even dreamed of.

She'd been totally innocent, but he'd been so gentle, so thorough, so—incredible—that she'd felt no pain, only joy and an unbelievable rightness.

Afterwards he walked her back, kissing her once more as he left her at the door of the farmhouse, his touch lingering.

Struck suddenly by some sense of evil, she pulled off her ring and gave it to him, pressing it into his hand.

'Here—have this. It was my grandmother's. It's a St Christopher. It will keep you safe.' And she reached up and kissed him again. 'Take care, my love,' she whispered, and his arms tightened for a second before he let her go.

He murmured something. She didn't really catch it. It sounded curiously like, *'Au revoir,'* but why would he be saying goodbye? So final, so irrevocable. It sent a shiver through her, and after she went to bed she lay and thought about it.

She must have misheard. It could have been *'Bonsoir'*, although even she knew that meant good evening and not goodnight. And anyway, he usually told her to sleep well. But *'Au revoir'*? Until we meet again? That seemed too final—not at all like goodnight. It puzzled her, but she convinced herself she must have heard it wrong, until the following day when she went down to make breakfast and found Madame Chevallier in tears.

A chill ran over her, and she hurried to her side, putting her arm around the woman who'd become her friend. *'Madame?'*

'Oh, Annie, *ma petite—je suis desolée.* I'm so sorry.'

'Pardon? Madame, what is it? What's happened?'

'Oh, *mon Dieu. C'est terrible.* Etienne—*il est mort!* Dead—*et* Gerard *aussi. Oh, mon Dieu!'*

Panic flooded her. Panic and the first terrible, overwhelming crush of grief. She sucked in a huge lungful of air, then another, fighting off the pain. 'No. You're wrong. You're lying! He can't be dead!'

But *Madame* shook her head and wept, her whole body shaken with sobs, and Annie realised it must be true.

'No... Dear God, no.'

She looked outside and saw the *gendarme* talking to Monsieur Gaultier, both of them shaking their heads in disbelief, and she ran out past them, up to the place where he'd taken her in his arms and made love to her with such passionate intensity just a few short hours before. Such exquisite joy—

'Etienne, no. You can't be dead,' she wept, falling to the soft, sweet earth where she'd lain with him so recently. 'No! It's not true.'

The sobs racked her body endlessly, the pain tearing her apart cell by cell, leaving her in tatters.

Madame found her there, prostrate with grief, and helped her back to the house.

'I have to go and see him,' she said. 'I can't believe—'

So Madame Chevallier called a taxi, and she went first to the village, but the *gendarme* wouldn't talk to her. Then she went to the town where it had happened, where the hospital was and the morgue, but the information was even less forthcoming.

The only thing she was sure of was that he was gone, but even his death she had to take on trust. She wanted to see his body, to say goodbye, but she was told his family had taken it already, and no, she couldn't be given their details.

'It is gone, *mademoiselle*. You cannot see him. You must go home.'

Home. It was the only thing in her suddenly topsy-turvy world to make sense. She'd go home, to the only people who really cared about her. Liz and Roger would look after her. She went back, packed her things and set off. She should have phoned them, but she couldn't bring herself to say the words, and so she made her way to Calais and took the first available crossing, caught the train from Dover and arrived back at ten that night, going straight to their house.

Roger answered the door, his face haggard, and Annie, even through her grief, could see that something was terribly, horribly wrong.

A shiver of dread ran down her spine. 'Roger?' she whispered. 'What's happened?'

'It's Liz,' he said, and then he started to cry, dry, racking sobs that tore her apart.

'Where is she?'

'In bed. Don't wake her. She's got a headache. Annie, she's dying—'

A brain tumour. Roger told her the bare bones, but Liz filled her in on all the details in the morning, sitting at the kitchen table after the children had gone to school.

'Inoperable?' she echoed hollowly. 'Are they sure?'

'Oh, yes. I've had every kind of scan, believe me.' Liz searched Annie's eyes, and frowned. Even then, in the midst of such agony, she noticed that something was wrong. Her hand found Annie's, gripping it hard. 'Annie, what is it? What's happened to you? You shouldn't be home yet. What's going on? You look awful, my love.'

She swallowed the tears, not wanting to cry about something that must seem so remote to this very dear friend in the midst of her own grief, but unable to hold them back. 'Etienne's dead.'

Liz's face was shocked. 'What? How? Why?'

She shook her head. 'I don't know. All they'd tell me was he'd been mugged in an alley in the town. He was with another man, and he was killed, too. They were beaten to death—'

'Who would do such a thing? Do they know who did it?'

She shook her head. 'I don't think so. They wouldn't tell me much. I just—Liz, I can't believe it. First him, and now you—'

And then the dam burst, and they held each other and wept the raw, bitter tears of grief...

The gravel crunched under his tyres as he drew to a halt, cut the engine and got out, a lump in his throat. He was about to ring the doorbell when an elderly terrier trotted round the corner of the house and came up to him, sniffing.

'Nipper?'

The dog pricked his ears, whined and jumped up at him, his stubby little tail thrashing wildly in apparent recognition, and the lump in his throat just got bigger.

'Nipper, it *is* you,' he murmured. 'I can't believe it! What a good old boy!' He crouched down, and the dog lashed his face with his tongue in greeting, all the time whining and wagging and wriggling furiously under his hands, unable to get enough of his old friend.

'Nipper! Nipper, get down! Bad dog. I'm so sorry. Nipper!'

He straightened slowly, taking in the changes that time had carved in his godmother's face. The lump wedged itself in his throat, so that for a moment he couldn't speak but could only stand there and let the homecoming fill his heart.

'I'm so sorry about that. What can I do for you?' she said, moving closer, and then suddenly she stopped, her hand flying to her mouth, the secateurs clattering unheeded to the ground at his feet. 'Michael?' she whispered soundlessly, and then recovered herself. 'I'm so sorry. For a moment there, I thought you were someone else—'

'Oh, Peggy, I might have known I wouldn't fool you,' he said gruffly, and he felt his face contort into a smile as his arms opened to receive her...

A river of tears later, they were sitting in the kitchen, his godmother on one side, his godfather on the other, catching up on nine very long years while the dog lay heavy on his feet, endlessly washing his ankle above the top of his sock as if he couldn't believe his old friend had really returned.

The dog wasn't alone. Peggy kept touching his face, her fingers infinitely gentle and tentative, getting to know the new him.

'It doesn't hurt,' he assured her quietly. Not much, at least. Not with the painkillers.

'But it did. It must have done.'

He nodded. 'Yes. It did. I'm glad you didn't see it.'

She shook her head. 'We should have been there for you.'

'It wasn't possible. It wasn't safe. I'm sorry they had to tell you I was dead.'

'I knew you weren't,' she told him. 'The flowers on my birthday, the cards. They said you were dead, but I knew.'

'I didn't believe her,' Malcolm said. 'I thought she was imagining it. At one point I thought she had a secret admirer—someone from the local horticultural society.'

'Silly man,' Peggy said with a fond smile. 'As if.' She paused, then went on, 'I don't suppose you can tell us—'

He gave a twisted smile. 'You know better than to ask that. I've told you all I can. It's all over the television, anyway—and all that really matters is that it's over and I'm alive—even if I don't really look like me any more.'

His godfather nodded wordlessly. 'If I may say so,' he muttered gruffly, 'the nose is better.'

He chuckled. 'I agree. The nose is a bonus. The headaches I could live without, and the teeth aren't great. At least they don't go in a glass at night, though, so I should be thankful for small mercies.'

'So—I take it they gave you a new identity? Who've you been all this time?'

'Michael Harding.'

'Oh—like the thriller writer. How ironic. I've read all his books…love 'em. Fancy you having the same name.'

'I *am* the writer,' he said diffidently, and shrugged. 'I had to do something while I was marking time, and I thought I might as well put all that experience to good use. I had no idea it was going to be such a success or that I'd love it so much.'

Peggy's eyes filled again and she nodded slowly. 'I wondered if it was you. I could hear your voice in the words. Oh, Michael, I'm so proud of you!'

Malcolm's hand curled round his shoulder, squeezing tight as he stood up. 'Absolutely. And your parents would have been proud—very, very proud, and with good reason. Many good reasons.'

'Thank you,' he said gruffly, unbearably touched. 'I'm just glad they didn't have to go through what you have done.'

'Amen to that.' He harrumphed and made a great production of clearing his throat. 'Well, I think this calls for a drink,' he said, retrieving a bottle of champagne from the fridge and putting three flutes on the table. He stripped off the foil and twisted the wire cage, just as Michael put his hand in his pocket.

'There's something else you should know,' he said, and pulled out a photograph and slid it on to the table. 'It seems I have a son.'

The cork popped loudly in the silence and, while the wine foamed unheeded over Malcolm's hand, Peggy started to weep again.

CHAPTER TWO

'GOOD morning.'

She looked up, and for a second her heart stopped.

And then he moved, stepped forwards into the room, and as the light hit his face Annie felt the stupid, foolish hope drain away and her heart started again.

She picked up a tea towel, drying her hands for something to do that didn't involve anything fragile like crockery. Crazy. For a moment there—but it was silly. It was just because she'd been thinking about him—

'You OK?' he asked, his voice low and rough and strangely sensuous. 'You look as if you've seen a ghost.'

She nearly laughed aloud, and dragged her eyes from the battered, lived-in face in front of her, staring down in bewilderment at her shaking hands. Lord, she should have stopped doing this after all these years, clutching at straws, seeing him in any random stranger, but there was just something—

'Sorry. You reminded me of someone. Can I get you anything?'

He shook his head. 'You must be Annie Miller. I'm Michael Harding—your landlord. It's good to meet you. I'm sorry it's taken so long.'

He held out his hand, and she dropped the tea towel and reached over the cakes and placed her hand briefly in his warm, strong grasp—a grasp that was somehow safe and solid and utterly reassuring.

She fought the urge to leave her hand there—probably for ever—and tried to remember how to talk.

'That's OK, I know you're busy. Ruth said you'd be coming over,' she told him, her voice unaccountably breathless. She retrieved her hand and found a smile from somewhere, and his lips tilted in answer, a crooked, distorted smile, one corner of his mouth strangely reluctant. It should have made him ugly, but it didn't, something about the eyes and firm, sculpted lips devastatingly attractive—

'Any chance of getting a few quiet minutes with you this morning so we can talk?' he was asking, his soft and yet rough voice doing something weird to her insides. She forced herself to concentrate on his words, and found herself suddenly nervous. Was this it? Was he going to give her notice? Planning to sell up or hike her rent out of reach?

She schooled her voice and her expression, trying to quell the panic. 'It's quiet now that the breakfast crowd have gone. Will this do?'

'Sure. I'd just like to chat, really—have a look round, see it with my own eyes. I haven't been here for years, but Ruth tells me you've done a good job. I gather it's very successful. I just wanted to make sure you're happy with everything.'

She felt the tension ease a fraction and wondered if she was being too trusting. Probably. It was her greatest fault.

'Help yourself, it won't take you long to see it all—the cloakroom's through that door at the back, and the store's out there too, and the kitchen you can see.'

He looked at it over the counter and nodded. 'Nice, having it in the middle like this. Friendly.'

'That was one of the things Liz and I insisted on, having the preparation area right in the middle of this long wall. It makes it relaxed and approachable, a bit like sitting in someone's kitchen while they cook for you. And you can see everything—there are no nasty surprises, no dirty corners. You know exactly what conditions your food's being prepared under, and people like that. We thought it was a good idea.'

He nodded. 'It's good. Low key, easy. Relaxed. I like it. Who's Liz?'

'Oh—the founder, really. She was my late husband's first wife. She was lovely.'

'Was?'

'She died nine years ago, just after she set it up.'

'I'm sorry,' he said, and for some reason it didn't seem like a platitude. He didn't dwell, though, but moved on, his eyes taking everything in, and she followed him, answering questions, smiling as necessary and wondering what he'd think of her housekeeping.

He went into the store, looked round, checked out the loo, then turned, almost on top of her, and her heart hitched.

'It is small, isn't it?' he said, far too close for comfort and trampling all over her common sense.

Ruth was right. He was broodingly sexy. Very. She backed away, reversing into a table. 'Intimate.'

'It's tiny,' he said, with a lopsided grin that made her heart lurch again.

'Small but perfectly formed,' she quipped, and his eyes flicked over her and returned to her face.

'Absolutely,' he murmured, and she stared into those gorgeous blue eyes and felt herself colour. Heavens. How could he not have been Ruth's type? He'd be any woman's type if she had a pulse—

She turned away abruptly. 'Coffee?' she said, her voice scratchy and a little high, and behind her she heard him clear his throat softly, more of a grunt than a cough, as if he was reining back, distancing himself from the suddenly intimate moment.

'That would be lovely.'

So she poured two mugs of coffee and set them down

on opposite sides of the round table by the window at the front, where she could see her regulars coming and get their orders under-way.

She took the chair closest to the kitchen area. 'I gather from Ruth that you want to refurbish the place,' she said, meeting those dazzling eyes head-on with a challenge, and he nodded.

'I do. It's looking a bit sad. I hadn't really registered—Ruth's been too uncomplaining, and so have you. The flat needs a new kitchen and bathroom, and with the antique shop empty I was thinking maybe we could do something more with this place—give you a little more room as well as freshening it up a little. If you want?'

'How much room?' she asked, trying to concentrate on the overheads and not his face. 'I can't really afford to pay much more.'

He shrugged, his lips pursing, one side reluctant. 'As much as you need. You could take all of it.'

She shook her head. 'The stairs would be in the way. I wouldn't like it divided into two—it wouldn't feel the same. And anyway, the kitchen's not big enough for all those tables. If you're offering bits of the place, I'd rather have the garden.'

He chuckled. 'How did I know that was coming?'

He peeled back the lid on the coffee creamer and tipped it in, stirring it with deliberation, and it gave her a moment to study him openly.

His hair was short and dark, the temples threaded with grey. She wondered how old he was. Forty? Forty-five? More, maybe, or less, but it seemed irrelevant. Whatever, he was very attractive in a very masculine and hard-edged way.

It was odd that he *was* so attractive, really, because his face wasn't classically handsome, by any means. There was something peculiar about it, she decided. Irregular. The jaw wasn't quite symmetrical, the left side of it etched with fine scars that carved white lines in the shadow of his stubble. His chin was a little crooked, his teeth not quite straight.

And yet it was an attractive face for all that. Interesting. She'd love to know the story behind it, but it wasn't the sort of thing you could ask.

Not yet, anyway. Maybe later, when she knew him better—and now she really *had* lost it! He was her landlord. This was their first meeting in seven years. Once the refurb was finished it would probably be another seven before she saw him again, and at that rate they'd both be dead before she knew him well enough to ask—

'Penny for them.'

She shook her head. No way! 'Nothing,' she denied. 'I was compiling a shopping list.'

One eyebrow arched. 'For a witch's brew?'

'I beg your pardon?'

'You were scowling at me. I don't think I fancy the recipe.'

She felt colour touch her cheeks. 'I'm sorry. I was miles away,' she lied.

Contemplating getting to know him better. Much better.

Oh, good grief! She hadn't done this for years, hadn't felt this devastating tug of attraction since—well, since Etienne.

Perhaps it was his body that had triggered the response? They were the same physical type—same height, or thereabouts, although Michael was heavier than Etienne. Same build, though—lithe and muscular. Powerful. And something about the eyes—

But it was more than that, something not quite physical, some deep connection that went right to the heart of her and tumbled her senses into chaos—just as Etienne had done, but in a very different way, because Etienne absolutely never brooded and Michael—well, Michael was deep as the ocean, and she could get lost in those eyes—

Then he looked up again, fixing her with those very eyes, and a slow, lazy curve tilted the right side of his mouth.

And the chaos just got worse.

Lord, she was gorgeous. Beautiful and defensive and responsive as ever, her skin colouring even as he looked at her.

That went with the auburn hair, of course, the rich, warm red that gave her those amazing green eyes and clear, creamy skin. She had freckles after the summer, just like she'd had in France—

He dragged his eyes away, coughed to clear his throat, hauled his libido back under control. He didn't want to blow it now, when it looked as though he'd got over the first hurdle. His heartbeat was starting to steady, the nerves of steel he'd always had before an op coming back now to help him through, but this was much, much harder, somehow much scarier because it was the real thing.

She'd given him a fright when she'd first looked up at him. He'd been sure she'd recognised him, but then she'd talked herself out of it as he watched. He'd seen the cogs turn, and then he'd just had to deal with her veiled curiosity.

She'd been studying him just now, and it had taken all his self-control not to get up and walk away. He hated looking like this—hated what had been done to him, the fact that he didn't recognise himself any more. And he hated being studied. Normally he would have walked away or stared the person down, but this was Annie, and she needed to be able to live with it. So he'd let her look, pretending interest in the coffee, just hoping it didn't make her want to run.

'So you want the garden?' he said, forcing himself to stick to the game plan, and for a moment she looked a little startled.

Then she nodded.

'Yes—but I know it goes with the flat.'

'Not necessarily,' he said slowly, watching her. 'We could certainly divide it. What did you have in mind? You've obviously been thinking about it—how long have you been here now, did you say?'

'Nine years.'

As if he didn't know that, almost to the minute. He kept his expression steady—not easy, considering. 'So in that time you must have come up with some ideas.'

'Oh, all sorts, but one of the problems is that to gain access to the garden at the back I'd have to lose one of the tables, and I can't really afford to do that. Our summers aren't reliable enough.'

'But you could have a conservatory.'

She laughed. 'I couldn't possibly justify the expense! It would cost a fortune to have one big enough to do any good, and the place doesn't do much more than break even really. I make a reasonable living, but I work hard for it and there's no slack in the system. I wouldn't contemplate taking on any expansion plans.'

'But I might.'

Her eyes snapped back to his, widening. 'Why? Why would you do that?'

He shrugged. Why, indeed? To make her happy? Crazy.

'I've got the money—why not? It would add to the value of the property.'

'Only if you're thinking of selling it,' she said, and he

could see the apprehension in her eyes. He shook his head and hastened to reassure her.

'No. It was just an idea. Don't worry about it. But the access to the cloakroom through the store—that's not a very good idea, and it's a bit cramped. There was a doorway on the other side at the back of the stairs, according to my plans. We could open it up and make a store there. Or create an alcove, as well as a store. Take more off the antique shop. There are lots of options. I don't see the cost as a factor. Think about it.'

She caught her lip between her teeth, worrying it gently, making it pinker. He had an overwhelming urge to soothe the tiny bruise with his tongue and had to remind himself firmly what he was doing here.

Helping. Not hindering, not chatting her up or flirting with her or putting the moves on her.

He'd done that nine years ago, and look where it had got them. No. This time he was going to do things right. Take it slowly, give them a chance to get to know each other properly. There was far too much at stake to blow it because of his over-active hormones.

He picked up his cup, dragged his eyes off her and drained it in one.

'Right. Let me pay you for the coffee and I'll go and get on. Lots to do.'

'Don't be ridiculous!' she said quickly. 'I wouldn't dream of taking any money off you—'

He laughed softly. 'No, I insist—because I'm just about to rip out the kitchen in the flat and I intend to pop down whenever I need a drink or something to eat, and if you won't let me pay my way I won't feel I can—'

'Rubbish. Anyway,' she said, and her mouth tipped up into a grin that made his heart crash against his ribs, 'I'll keep a tally and get my pound of flesh. I'm still after the garden, remember?'

He laughed again, and shook his head. 'I won't argue—for now. And think about what I said about the changes you want.'

'I will. Thanks.'

She met his eyes, and the urge to bend forwards and brush his lips against hers nearly overwhelmed him.

Nearly.

He slotted the chair under the table, grabbed his jacket and fled for the door before he got himself into trouble.

Wow.

Annie sat down again with a bump, staring after him. The door at the bottom of the stairs closed softly behind him, and she heard his footsteps running up into the flat above. Suddenly she could breathe again, and she sucked in a great lungful of air and shook her head to clear it.

Wow, she thought again. What *was* it about him? Was it simply that he'd reminded her so forcefully of Etienne? Although he wasn't really that like him. It had just been the initial shock.

But it was more than the looks. He had the same way of concentrating on what she was saying, really listening to her, watching her attentively. Etienne had done that, and it had made her feel somehow special.

Crazy. Michael was just trying to find out what she wanted from the tearoom. He wasn't being attentive; he was just listening to her suggestions for improving his investment.

And any fanciful notions to the contrary had better go straight out of her head, together with any foolish ideas about getting to know him better. This minute.

Now.

There was a thump upstairs, and her attention zinged straight back to him.

Great, she thought. Kept your mind off him for less than a second. You're doing well, Annie. Really well.

There was another thump overhead. With any luck he'd be so busy up there he wouldn't find time to come down here pestering her and putting her senses into turmoil.

'You need a life,' she muttered. 'One half-decent man wanders in here and you go completely to pieces.'

She put the scones in the oven, straightened up and saw a coach pull into the square. Oh, no! Just what she needed when her brain was out to lunch. She threw a few more scones into the pan, shut the oven door and refilled the coffee machine as the first of the coach party wandered through the door, peered around and headed for the window table.

Plastering on a smile, she picked up her notepad and went out into the fray.

He'd done it.

Amazing.

OK, theirs had been a brief affair, and nine years would have blurred the memories, but even so he was surprised he'd got away with it.

He shouldn't have been. It was no surprise, really. The young Frenchman she'd loved was dead. She wouldn't be looking for him in an Englishman, especially one who looked so different. When he'd caught her studying him, the look on her face had caught him on the raw. There was no way there'd been recognition in her eyes, just curiosity, and maybe a little fascination. He didn't want her to be fascinated—at least, not like that, but he couldn't blame her. He was no oil painting.

Apart from the nerve damage that had taken away the

spontaneous little movements of his lips, contorting his smile, the structure had been so damaged that, even if she'd known, she would have struggled to recognise him. Hell, he sometimes had a shock even now when he caught sight of himself in a mirror. Not to mention the fact that it had aged him more than he cared to admit. He sure as hell didn't look like a man of thirty-eight.

Of course his stupid masculine pride had hoped she'd recognise him right away, and there'd been that moment of panic when she'd first seen him. He'd got away with it, though, brazened it out, and the bit of him that still had any common sense knew it was just as well.

What he wanted—no, needed—was time to build a relationship with her as the people they were now.

No strings. No past. Just the present.

And hopefully the future...

And this place would give him all the time he needed. Whistling softly under his breath, he found a screwdriver and set about dismantling the cupboards.

He hadn't been exaggerating about using her as a kitchen.

He came down for coffee at eleven-thirty, then reappeared at one looking scruffy and harassed and short of caffeine.

'I could do with some lunch,' he said gruffly.

'Coffee first?' she said with a smile that wouldn't quite behave, and he gave her that lopsided grin that creased his eyes and turned her insides out, and nodded.

'You'd better believe it—a huge one—and something substantial to blot it up following not far behind. I'm starving.'

'A pasta bake with roasted vegetables and a side salad?'

'Chuck in a good big lump of bread and you're on.'

She suppressed the smile, but it wouldn't quite go. 'Bad day?'

'The kitchen's fighting back,' he said drily, showing her his hand, and she tutted and cleaned up the scuff on his knuckle with a damp paper napkin and stuck a plaster on it.

'Thanks,' he murmured, then added cheekily, 'I'll get out of your way now—I'd hate to hold up my lunch,' and looked around for a table.

She felt her eyebrows shoot up and a smile tugged at her lips. 'Pushing your luck, aren't you? We're a bit busy—sit by the window with the others. It's my regulars' table—I think you probably qualify already and it's all you deserve after that remark, so I'm throwing you to the piranhas!'

'Are they that bad?'

She laughed. 'You don't know the half of it.'

He chuckled and went over, introducing himself to them and settling his lean, rangy body on the only spare chair. By the time she'd poured his coffee and put the pasta bake in the microwave to heat, he was already entrenched in their conversation about parking on the market square, the current hot topic in the village.

She pulled up the little stool she used for reaching the top of the fridge-freezer and joined them for a few moments, content just to sit there and watch them all wrangling over the insoluble problem of conservation versus trade.

Michael wasn't having that, though. He turned to her and said, 'So what's your opinion?' and dragged her into the conversation.

She laughed and threw up her hands. 'I don't have one. Well, to be exact, I have two, so I don't count. When I'm here, I want people to be able to park. When I'm at home, which is there—' she pointed out her house to him through the window '—I don't want to look at cars. So I'm keeping out of it, not that it will make the slightest difference, because the council will do what they think fit and ignore us all as usual—'

Grace chipped in with her ferociously held views on conservation, Chris complained that there was never anywhere to park close enough to leave a sleeping baby in the vehicle for a few minutes to grab a sanity-restoring coffee amongst friends, and Michael cradled his coffee in his big battered hands and sat back and smiled at her over the pandemonium.

Good grief. How intimate that smile seemed in the crowded room. And how curious that his smile should have become so important to her in such a ridiculously short space of time! The microwave beeped, rescuing her from mental paralysis and any further dangerous speculation, and she leapt up and went back into her little kitchen area and made his salad and sliced him a couple of big chunks of corn bread, her whole body humming with the awareness of his eyes on her for the entire time.

She set the plate down in front of him, warned him that the pasta bake would be hot, and went back behind her counter to deal with a customer who was leaving and wanted to pay the bill.

Then another couple came in and dithered about and changed their order half a dozen times, sat down, glanced across at Michael's meal and changed their minds again.

By the time she'd dealt with them, cleared a couple of tables and loaded the dishwasher, her regulars were drifting out and Michael was left at the table on his own. He wandered over, coming into the kitchen area that was strictly off limits to customers, and when she pointed that out to him he told her calmly that he owned it and anyway, even if he didn't, she wasn't clearing up after him.

And he put his plate in the dishwasher, refilled his coffee mug and looked round at her crowded little workspace with a pleated brow. 'Poky, isn't it?'

'It's efficient.'

'No, it isn't. It's outdated and cramped.'

'It was the best we could afford,' she said, beginning to bristle and wondering what had happened to that smile that melted her insides, when he suddenly produced it.

'And you've done wonders with it, and you're clearly hugely popular, but that's not a surprise,' he said softly in the low, gravelly voice that finished what the smile had started. 'That pasta bake was delicious. Thank you.'

He sighed and raked his fingers through his hair, the smile rueful now. 'Unfortunately the kitchen's still waiting for me upstairs, so I suppose I ought to go and tackle it before I start rearranging yours. Come and sit and have a drink with me for a minute first, though,' he said, and all the reasons why she shouldn't suddenly went out of the window.

She sat down, pushed the regulars' wreckage out of the way for a moment, and buried her nose in a much-needed cup of coffee. 'Oh, bliss,' she murmured.

'Hectic morning?'

'I haven't stopped,' she confessed. 'It's been bedlam. I was going to have a look through a few recipe books for some new soups, but I haven't had a chance.'

'You do soup?'

She nodded. 'In the winter. I'll be starting it any day now. It's really popular, but I like to do a variety and introduce a few new ones every year. I used to test them out on Roger, but since he died I have to test them on my customers—dangerous, if it bombs!'

'You could test them on me,' he offered, and her heart skittered crazily. Why? They were talking about sampling soups, nothing more. Certainly nothing that should make her heart dance about like a manic puppet!

'You're just after more food,' she said, trying to lighten the suddenly electric atmosphere.

He sat back and chuckled. 'Of course. If I play my cards right, I won't ever have to cook at all. What could be better?'

She was saved the necessity of finding a reply by the arrival of customers, and while she was sorting out their order, Michael left, waggling his fingers at her as he went out of the door and headed up the stairs.

There was a thump and a crash, followed by something she was glad she and her customers couldn't quite hear, and his footsteps came back down the stairs again.

'Got another plaster?' he asked, and she threw him the first aid kit.

'Take it with you—you're obviously going to need it,' she said with a smile, and thus cleverly avoided having to touch him. She was still tingling from the last time!

His finger was sore.

Not that he was any stranger to pain, far from it, but it was just constantly in the way. Everything seemed to require pressure on just that bit of the pad that he'd sliced on the hinge, and finally he packed up his tools, looked around at the carnage and headed back downstairs.

Time for a bucketful of tea, something tasty from her selection of mouthwatering cakes to tide him over until he could be bothered to cook later, and another opportunity to get close to the woman who'd dominated his life and his thoughts for so long.

You're overdoing it, he told himself, but he didn't seem to have any control, and when he walked in her eyes flicked up and caught his instantly and she smiled, and his heart slammed against his ribs and hiccuped into a nice steady gallop.

Nine years, he thought, and he still felt just the same. Time to cool off. Fast.

'I'm going home—I know when I'm beaten. I'll see you tomorrow,' he said and, resisting the urge to hang around any longer, he headed for the door, just as a small boy dragging a backpack wandered in.

'Hi, Mum,' he said, and Annie gave the boy a smile that melted Michael's aching heart.

'Hi, darling. Good day at school?'

Damn. If only he hadn't said he was going—

Whatever. He'd waited over eight years for a formal introduction to his son. Another day or two wouldn't make any difference. He forced himself to carry on walking…

'Mummy, you aren't *listening* to me!'

She jumped guiltily, put down the iron and switched her attention back to Stephen—and away from the man who'd been occupying altogether too much time in her head for the past ten hours.

Heavens, was that all it was? Ten short hours? It seemed—

'Mumm-eeee!'

'Sorry, darling. What is it?'

'My French homework. I can't do it.'

French. She gave a strangled little laugh. Her French was appalling—just enough to get her in trouble, and not enough to get her out of it.

No. Don't go there.

She looked at the book opened out on her kitchen table, and felt a flutter of panic. 'Darling, I'm sorry, my French isn't up to much. Is it easy?'

'If it was easy, I wouldn't need you to help me,' he said

in that tone of voice that eight-year-olds reserved for people who were particularly intellectually challenged. 'My father would have been able to help me,' he added with an elaborate sigh.

'Daddy wasn't any better at French than me,' she pointed out, but Stephen just looked at her patiently.

'No, not *Daddy*, my *father*.'

Etienne.

Heavens, how he was cropping up in her life in the last few days! She'd hardly thought of him for years, and now here he was again.

'Yes, he would have been able to help you,' she said, her voice a little strained. 'I'm sorry I'm so useless.' Useless and exhausted and unable to think of anything but Etienne and…inexplicably—the broodingly sexy Michael.

'You aren't useless,' Stephen said kindly. 'Just bad at French. But it's OK, I still love you and you make great cakes.'

She smiled and ruffled his hair, making him duck out of her reach and swat her hand away.

'What's a window?'

'*La fenêtre,*' she told him.

'Why's it a girl? That's silly.'

But he wrote it down, checking the spelling, his tongue poking out of the side of his mouth as he struggled with the unfamiliar word. 'What's a door?'

'*La porte,*' she said automatically, getting up to answer the phone and hoping desperately that whoever was ringing was good at French, or at least better than her. 'Ruth—hi! How are things?'

'Great. Fantastic. I should have done it ages ago.'

Annie smiled, pleased for her friend and feeling only a little twinge of envy. 'I'm really glad,' she said, squashing the green streak firmly. 'You deserve a good man in your life.'

'Talking of which, how did you get on today with Michael? Did he come over?'

Her heart did that now-familiar tap-dance on her ribcage, and her mouth kicked up a notch. 'Oh, yes. He's torn the place apart, judging by the noise and the language overhead and the number of plasters he's had off me.'

Ruth laughed. 'So he hasn't put your rent up yet?'

She chuckled. 'No. In fact, if anything, he keeps trying to foist new bits of the premises on to me—the antique shop, more room for a store—'

'Well, let's face it, Annie, you could do with the extra space.'

'Yes, but not the extra cost, which incidentally he's being extraordinarily evasive about. And he keeps pointing out how crowded and poky it is, and I'm beginning to wonder if he isn't right.'

'He is right—and that's part of the charm of the place. Tell him you like it as it is. Have the store, because you need it, but nothing else if you don't want it. Don't let him bully you. Be firm, for goodness' sake, or he'll railroad you into all sorts. I know him, remember. He's like a steamroller when he gets going and he'll kill you with kindness. I should know.'

'I'll bear it in mind. How's your French?'

'Awful.' She hesitated for a second. 'What's the problem?'

'Stephen's homework,' she said. 'He's eight and I can cope now, but I'll be out of my depth in a week! And another thing—now you've moved away I can't test my soups on you,' she added in mock protest. 'Are you sure Tim's so great?'

Ruth laughed. 'Absolutely! And if you want a guinea pig

for your soup, ask Michael. Wait till he's pressuring you about the premises and slip it in to distract him. Food's the easiest way to divert him, because he always forgets to eat and he's always hungry.'

'Well, he was certainly hungry today, he had loads—and he's already volunteered for the soup-testing detail.'

'He didn't waste any time, then. I bet you're spoiling him. You don't want to do that, he'll get fat.'

Annie chuckled. 'I'll tell him you said that. And you take care. Come and see me some time.'

'I will. I might bring Tim at the weekend.'

'Do that. Speak soon.'

She hung up and turned back to Stephen, to find him engrossed in a book, his homework forgotten.

'Hey, you, come on. French.'

'Finished it.'

'Really?'

'Really. Can we have ice cream?'

'Not till you've put your books away. Are you sure you've finished?'

He rolled his eyes, and there was such a look of his father about him that her heart hiccuped. Crazy. She hadn't thought about him in ages, and now it seemed she couldn't think about anything else.

Except Michael, and even that was confusing.

She dreamed about Etienne that night, laughing softly in the darkness, kissing her under the spreading branches of the old oak behind the château—but when he turned his head in the moonlight, he had Michael's face, and she woke hot and breathless and aching for something she'd almost forgotten existed...

CHAPTER THREE

HE WAS already upstairs thumping around and laying waste to the flat by the time she opened up at twenty to nine.

Grace was one of the first in, followed by Chris and then Jackie.

'So, what's this with the landlord, then?' Chris asked, her eyes bright with curiosity.

'What's what? He's doing up the flat—you can hear it.'

'Hmm. We aren't blind, we all noticed,' Grace told her, which meant they'd been talking about it at some point since lunchtime yesterday.

She slapped some bacon into the electric griddle and sighed. 'Now look, girls, let's get one thing straight. He's my landlord—nothing more, nothing less.'

'You were being very nice to him.'

She rolled her eyes. 'Grace, of course I was being nice to him. I'm hardly going to alienate myself from him, am I?'

'Alienate yourself from who?' Michael asked, strolling in as if he owned the place—funny, that—and grinning at her, so that there was nothing to do but brazen it out, and serve them all right.

'You. They think there's something going on between us, because they have such sad little lives they have to gossip about something—'

'Sorry, ladies, she's right. Nothing's going on,' he assured them, and then ruined it by adding, 'sadly. However, while there's life…' His mouth quirked. 'Have I just ruined my chances of getting breakfast?'

52

She could cheerfully have hit him. Her heart, however, had other ideas, and seemed to be connected directly to her mouth, which promptly smiled forgivingly. Her tongue, however, was still her own.

'That depends on whether you're going to sit quietly and behave, or incite this lot to riot, because believe me, they need no encouragement,' she said tartly.

'As if I'd do that,' he said, cosying up to them all and grinning that curiously engaging crooked grin of his.

'So, what are you doing upstairs? Apart from making lots of very impressive noises, that is,' Jackie said, leaning towards him and showing him too much cleavage for comfort. Well, Annie's comfort, anyway. Michael was probably feeling just fine, she thought acidly.

He grunted. 'I'm glad you're impressed. The kitchen doesn't seem to think I'm being in the least effective.'

He held out his damaged hands, and they clucked and tutted and fussed over him like a flock of broody hens until she could have hit them.

'Breakfast,' she said, setting down a huge heap of bacon sandwiches in the middle of the table, followed by a jug of coffee, a pot of tea and a handful of mugs.

The heap vanished in seconds, mostly into Michael.

'Ruth told me not to overfeed you,' she said blandly, and he snorted.

'She's a hard woman,' he murmured.

'She said you'd get fat.'

He laughed then—not the huge, all-encompassing laugh that Etienne would have laughed, or Roger's dry chuckle, but a quiet huff of laughter that for some reason made her feel sad.

She didn't know why, but something gave her the feeling that he didn't laugh much, that perhaps he didn't know how, or had forgotten.

Silly, really, when she looked at the easy way he was getting on with her friends, but there was just something—

'So how *is* the kitchen?'

'Winning. I might take a sledgehammer to it.' He drained his coffee, pushed back his chair and stood up. 'In fact, I think I'll do that now, teach it a lesson. See you all later.'

'And I need to get back and fight with the washing machine,' Chris said dolefully. 'I know—perhaps I'll take a sledgehammer to that. Solve the problem for a few days, anyway! Perhaps then I'd get to dawdle here all morning like you lot while my daughter's at nursery!'

Annie put the plates in the dishwasher, wiped the table and topped up the coffee before sitting down again with Jackie and Grace. 'Right, you two,' she said briskly, to keep them off the subject of her destructive and altogether too interesting landlord. 'Soup recipes. What works, what doesn't?'

'I like your parsnip soup,' Grace said promptly.

Jackie pulled a face. 'I don't. I like the winter vegetable—it's easier to see what's in it. The parsnip's just a purée.'

'Didn't like the minestrone you tried last year,' Grace continued. 'The broccoli and Stilton was good, though. Try that again.'

'Mmm—yes. I'd forgotten that. What about carrot and orange?' Annie suggested.

'In stick-in-the-mud old Suffolk? They'll hate it, too weird,' Jackie said, instantly damning the entire county.

Predictably, Grace bristled. 'That's unfair and a sweeping generalisation. And anyway, there's nothing wrong with sticking to tradition. I think you should try it instead of doing things differently just for the hell of it,' Grace said.

'Oh, Lord, I've poked a sleeping tiger. Little Miss Let's Preserve It At All Costs is up in arms—ouch!'

'Serve you right,' Grace said. 'I'll give you poking tigers. Annie, if you want to try carrot and orange, by all means do so. Why don't you try it out on Michael?'

'And talking of Michael—'

'We were talking about soup,' she reminded them.

'So we were. I wonder whose idea that was?' Grace murmured.

'Not mine—I can think of *much* more interesting things to talk about,' Jackie replied with a cheeky grin. 'Starting with that very, *very* sexy man upstairs. Any more coffee?'

He could hear the laughter underneath, and it was curiously comforting to know that her life wasn't all just one continuous grind to make ends meet.

Her friends were nice people. Good people, caring, if a little over-curious. They'd look out for her.

And watch him, clearly, like hawks. Well, that was fine. He wasn't intending to do anything wrong, but their courtship was clearly going to be a more public and open thing than he'd anticipated, and when he told her the whole story—well, there'd be the whole village lined up to hear the tale, no doubt, and judge him accordingly.

Damn.

He didn't go down for lunch. Instead he slowly and systematically dismantled the kitchen units, ripped up the carpets and ordered a skip. The rest of the day was spent trekking up and down the stairs with armfuls of rubbish, and by the time he'd filled the skip he was feeling shaky with hunger and he'd got a killer headache coming on.

But he didn't want to go in there until Stephen got off the school bus, and it was nearly six before he accepted that Tuesdays were clearly different.

He was crouched down packing up his tools for the night

when he heard a light footfall on the stairs and Annie appeared in the doorway of the kitchen.

'Hi—I hope you don't mind me coming up.'

He turned and sat against the wall, stretching out his cramped legs and sighing. 'Not at all. Come in.'

'I just wondered—you haven't been in since breakfast. I hoped it wasn't because of what I said about Ruth telling me not to feed you too much.'

He gave a wry smile. Well, they all looked wry these days, or awry, anyway, but this one at least was meant to. 'I just wanted to get the place cleared. I didn't really think to stop,' he lied, and she tutted.

'Ruth said you often forget to eat. I wondered—Stephen's at chess club at school tonight until seven, and he's being dropped off by a friend's mother after she's fed them. It'll be about eight o'clock, and I was going to play with a soup recipe. I've also got some leftover bits of quiche that are destined for the bin if they aren't eaten today. Can I tempt you?'

'Don't you want to go home?' he asked, unwilling to admit even to himself how horribly tempted he was, but she flashed him a tentative smile.

'Oh, I am going home,' she said. 'Sorry, I didn't make that clear. I wondered if you wanted to come over—but I expect you've got better things to do.'

He jack-knifed to his feet, dusting off his seat and trying not to look too damned eager.

'Not at all. I can't think of anything I'd rather do.'

'In which case you can carry the bag with all the dishes in it for me.' She grinned, and headed for the door.

Flicking off the lights, he followed her down, locked the door of the flat and slung the strap of the bag she handed him over his shoulder. 'Just lead the way,' he said.

They went in through the back door, over a mat that said

'Beware of the Kids'. That made him smile, till he remembered one of them was his. Then he felt a strange pang somewhere in the middle of his chest.

A large ginger cat was lying on the windowsill, paws tucked under his chest, and he turned his head and studied the newcomer with baleful eyes.

'Nice cat.'

'He's a horrible cat. He rules the house. Stephen's the only one he'll tolerate, and he'll let him do anything. He drapes him round his neck like a collar and the cat just lies there. If I try and stroke him he shreds me, so be warned. Stick that there—thanks.'

He set the bag down, and she put the kettle on, told him to sit down and started putting the contents of the bag away and pulling things out of the fridge.

'So—what's the soup going to be?' he asked, to take his mind off the sight of black trousers stretched taut over a firm, slender bottom that was doing unspeakable things to his fragile self-control.

'Don't know. I'll see what I've got. I like to use seasonal vegetables, but that can be a bit restricting, so I have to put unusual things in, like nuts and spices and stuff. I've made a Stilton and broccoli soup that goes down well, and there are the usual standbys, but I just fancied doing something unusual.'

'How about Jerusalem artichokes?'

'Fiddly to peel.'

'My godmother doesn't peel them; she scrubs them and cooks them in with onions and something else—can't remember what, but it's gorgeous. Spinach, maybe. I know it's green. Want me to ask her?'

Annie nodded. 'Could you? That would be really kind.'

'No problem,' he murmured, stretching out his legs and easing the kinks in his body while he watched her.

She made a cup of tea and set it down in front of him, then started chopping and slicing.

'Anything I can do?'

'Sit there and talk to me.'

'OK.'

But where to start? So many questions to ask, so much he wanted to know. This one he knew, but he thought it might get him other answers, answers to the questions he couldn't ask. 'Why a tearoom?' he said, and waited.

'Oh. Well, that goes back years, to Roger's first wife—Liz. I was telling you about her. Roger was my husband—you met him once. You probably don't remember.'

'Of course I do. He was incredibly generous about my writing. I was sorry to hear he'd died.'

'Thank you. He liked you—said you were very interesting. I was out at the time—you popped in because Ruth had said he liked your books. You brought him a signed copy—it's in his study, in pride of place. He treasured it.'

Guilt washed over him. He'd only done it so he could see the man she'd married, talk to him and find out what kind of man was bringing up his son.

Decent, had been the answer. Decent and straightforward and endlessly kind, and he'd felt relieved and guilty at the same time. Not to mention jealous as hell.

'You were saying about Liz,' he said, dragging the conversation back on track, and she nodded.

'She was a tutor at college—I got to know her quite well during my course, and we became friends. She was fed up with lecturing, though, and since her girls were growing up she felt she could take on something else, with commitment in the holidays.'

'Hence the tearoom?'

Annie nodded. 'She suggested we got together and started a little business, and we talked about it, and then the lease on that one came up. It was ideal, so handy for her, and I wasn't very far away. It had always been a little café, but it had a dreadful reputation and it was in dire need of sorting out. We ripped out the kitchen, rearranged and refitted it and were going to open in the autumn.'

'Not the best time, surely?'

'Well, not really, but with all the work to do on it we wouldn't have been ready for the summer, and I was already committed to going to France for September and October—I'd got a job cooking for the harvest season on a vineyard in the Rhône valley, to get some experience of French country cooking—not the fancy, twiddly stuff I'd done at college but real, proper food. And we thought the winter would give us time to find our feet.'

'And did it?'

'We never got the chance to find out. We decided Liz should open it when school started, working on the principle that business would take a while to pick up and it wouldn't be too busy until I got back, and that way Liz could have the last summer holiday with her children. We didn't realise it was going to be her last summer ever.'

She broke off, not saying any more, and he waited a while before prompting her.

'What happened?' he said softly, and she lifted a shoulder in the way he remembered so well and carried on, her voice quiet and slightly expressionless.

'She had a brain tumour. She died that February. She'd already opened Miller's, of course, while I was away, and I ended up running it and looking after her and the girls, but it wasn't easy, not when I was pregnant as well.'

His heart hitched against his ribs. Now he was getting somewhere. 'Pregnant?' he said carefully. 'That wasn't on the agenda, was it?'

Her laugh was gentle but self-deprecating. 'Not exactly.

France was—a disaster. I fell in love with one of the estate managers, a guy called Etienne Duprés—stupid, stupid thing to do, but I was young and impressionable and he was gorgeous—good-looking, virile, sweep-you-off-your-feet type. He certainly swept me off mine.'

'So Roger wasn't Stephen's father?'

She shook her head. 'No—good heavens, no. He was married to Liz—devoted to her.'

'Sorry. I just assumed Stephen had come along later, after you were married,' he lied, and wondered why he didn't choke on it.

'No. He was Etienne's child.'

And stupidly, hearing her actually say the words meant an enormous amount. Even though he knew—had concrete proof, in fact—that Stephen was his child, to hear her acknowledge it gave him a curious sense of satisfaction.

'So why didn't you marry this Etienne guy?' he prompted, and held his breath. What would she say? What did she know? He wasn't sure. All he'd been able to find out was that she'd returned to England and had a child. His child. So he held his breath and watched her carefully. Even so, he almost missed the flicker of pain in her eyes.

'He died. He and another man who worked with him. They were beaten up. Their bodies were found a few miles away in the town. I never did know why—I don't suppose there was a reason, but the French authorities stonewalled me when I tried to find out more. They must have known something was going on, I suppose. It was on the news the other day, the vineyard—something to do with human trafficking. I don't know if you saw it.'

He shrugged, wondering what she'd say, how she'd felt about seeing it. He knew how he'd felt—sick, for the most part.

'Rings a bell. What about it?' he said casually.

'Claude Gaultier—he was the owner—was running some kind of slave labour and prostitution racket. He was a gangmaster, I think is the term. I suspect Etienne and his friend must have got themselves involved somehow.'

Clever girl. 'Wrong place, wrong time?' he murmured, watching her carefully still, and she nodded.

'Maybe. It might have been nothing to do with it, of course; I could just be letting my imagination run away with me. Anyway, I never got a chance to see his body. They said it had been taken away by his family. So that was it. For a while I thought I'd die, too, but you don't, do you? You just go on, day by day, on autopilot. I came back, found that Liz was terminally ill and got on with it.'

'And then you married Roger,' he said, and waited.

She hesitated for a moment. 'Yes. He was a wonderful man—a brilliant father, even though he was ill. I never thought I'd get over Etienne, but he helped me to see that there was more than one kind of love.'

'You miss him.'

It wasn't a question, but she answered it anyway, turning the knife a little further. 'Roger?' she said, and smiled tenderly. 'Yes, I miss him. Every day.' And then she added unexpectedly, 'Sometimes I'm so lonely, and I wonder if this is all there is now, all there's going to be—'

She broke off, colouring. 'I can't believe I'm telling you this,' she muttered, turning back to her chopping board. She attacked the vegetables, slicing and chopping them viciously and scraping them into a big pot. Then, throwing in a slosh of olive oil, she turned on the heat and started to stir them, all without saying another word.

He waited her out, nursing his tea and watching her while he dealt with the fact that she still missed this man who'd taken what should have been his place in her life, and after a few minutes she crumbled a stock cube into the mix, poured water over the top and came and sat down.

'I'm sorry. I don't normally dish out personal information like that,' she said at last, but she wouldn't meet his eyes, and with a quiet sigh he reached out a finger and tilted up her chin, forcing her to face him.

'It's OK,' he murmured. 'You've been through hell in the last few years. You needed to let off steam, and it's going nowhere. I don't gossip.'

She coloured again, nodded and found a little smile. 'Thanks.'

'Any time. How old are you, Annie? Late twenties, early thirties?'

The smile faltered. 'Thirty.'

'And you're alone,' he murmured, hearing his voice turn husky. 'That's such a travesty. You should have a lover, Annie—someone to share the nights with.'

The colour returned in force, but she met his eyes defiantly. 'So who do you share your nights with, Michael? I've never heard Ruth talk about a Mrs Harding.'

He gave a huff of laughter. Oh, he shared his nights, all right—with the woman opposite him, in his dreams. But there was no way she was knowing that, not yet. '*Touché*. You've got me there. But I'm different. I'm used to it. It's my choice.'

She studied him thoughtfully. 'Is it? Or are you just as lonely as anybody else?'

He held her eyes with effort. 'I don't see it as loneliness,' he lied. 'I prefer the word solitude. It helps me write.' But she just arched a brow and went back to her soup while the tension hummed between them like a bow-string.

He forced himself to relax, to take a nice, steady breath, to drink his tea.

'Thought any more about the alterations?' he said at last,

and she paused in her stirring and tasting and looked at him over her shoulder, spoon poised over the pot.

'Not really. I just wish I knew what your motives were.'

No way, he thought. He was going to hell for this and all the other lies he was telling her just now, but there was no help for it. 'No motives,' he said evenly. 'I just want to keep my tenants happy, and now seems a good time to make changes, with you the only one it affects.'

She gave him a doubtful look, sloshed something into the soup and stirred, tasted again and put the lid on.

'I could do with more storage.'

'OK.'

'And the garden, if I could see a way. And the alcove you were talking about.'

'Or you could move the whole thing next door into the antique shop, fit its store room out as a kitchen and have loads of room, and a door to the garden.'

She blinked and sat down opposite him as if her strings had been cut.

'Move it next door?'

He shrugged. 'Whatever. It's possible at the moment to do anything. That's all I'm saying. Think out of the box.'

Her smile was wry. 'Michael, I can't afford to think out of the box.'

'I could go in with you.'

'What—take turns to make soup and cakes and load the dishwasher? I don't think so.'

'I could be a silent partner.'

'I don't need someone else sharing the profits. I don't make enough as it is.'

'You might make more with more room.'

'It would lose its intimacy. I think that would be a mistake. And anyway, I'm running at full stretch as it is. I only get help for a few hours on some days. I can't afford to expand.'

'You should charge more. You're too cheap. You could add fifty per cent—'

'And lose all my regulars? I don't think so.'

He conceded the point, prodding the issue around a little further just for the sake of hearing her voice. He didn't care what she did about the business. He hoped, rashly, that it would all be academic in a few weeks anyway, if his plan worked out.

She stood up again, tested the soup, poured it into a liquidiser, tested it again, stirred in something that looked suspiciously like cream and set the bowl down on the table between them.

'So what is it?'

She shrugged. 'Winter vegetable medley?' she suggested with a grin, and he chuckled.

'Winging it?'

'Absolutely. Just wanted to try a few new flavours. It's a sweet potato base—that's where the colour comes from. I tell you what, if it's OK I'll let you name it.'

'You'll have to try harder than that to get the garden,' he growled softly, and she laughed.

He held out his bowl to her, struggling to regain control of his emotions. Her laugh had haunted him, a light-hearted ripple of sound that he hadn't heard for years, and it went straight to his heart.

He put the bowl down, watched her as she ladled some into her own bowl and then looked at him expectantly.

'Well, go on then—taste it,' she prompted, but he shook his head.

'After you,' he said, his voice a little tight and gruff, but it was a miracle he could talk at all. He certainly couldn't eat. The soup had to wait a moment until he'd shifted the lump in his throat.

*   *   *

It seemed so odd having a man in her kitchen again. No, scratch that. It seemed odd having a man like this in her kitchen. At all. Ever.

Roger had never made her feel like this, not even remotely. He'd never threatened her physical space, never crowded her, never made her aware of every hair on her head and every inch of her body.

Not that Michael was doing anything to make her nervous. He didn't have to. He just had to sit there and breathe, and it was enough.

Crazy. She'd only ever felt like this once before, and she'd been twenty-one and innocent. Now she was thirty—and only marginally less innocent, she conceded. Still, she dealt with flirts every day in her work, and never had a problem.

Michael hardly flirted, though. He just talked to her, watched her working, focused on her with that *intensity* that was so darned unnerving. And he seemed to have an extraordinary capacity to get her to spill her guts.

She couldn't *believe* what she'd told him. Too much information, she thought. Crazy woman. You'll frighten him away.

And suddenly, she realised that that mattered, much, much more than it should have done.

'Is it OK?' she asked, to fill the deafening silence, and he nodded.

'Excellent.'

He'd seemed reluctant to start eating, but once he had, his spoon dipped rhythmically into the soup and she refilled his bowl twice before he put the spoon down with careful deliberation and shot her a wry grin.

'That was delicious. Thank you.'

'Name?'

He chuckled, making shivers run over her skin. 'You'll

have to give me time. How about Annie's Winter Warmer?'
he suggested after a moment, his head cocked on one side
and his eyes fixed on her face.

She shrugged. 'Could do. Mmm. Yeah, maybe—all I
have to do is remember what I put in it.'

No mean achievement considering she hadn't been able
to concentrate!

'Quiche?' she suggested, wondering if he'd be able to fit
anything else in, but he nodded.

'Please. I'm starving.'

'Still?'

He laughed softly, rippling her senses. 'I've been working hard. There's a lot of me.'

'I noticed,' she said, but she didn't explain which bit of
his remark she was referring to, and thankfully he had the
sense not to ask.

Instead he looked down at the table, lining up his bowl
and mug and knife with careful precision, and she grabbed
the chance to move without him watching her and stood
up, clearing the table and bringing out the last few slices
of quiche.

'There are two sorts. If I put it all out, you can choose.'

'You're not having any?' he asked, but she shook her
head.

'I'm full. I had a scone earlier. I need to make some
things for tomorrow, but you carry on, please.'

And if she didn't have to sit opposite him she might have
some chance of slowing her heartbeat down before it went
off the scale...

So what had she noticed?

The fact that he'd been working hard, or the fact that
there was a lot of him?

Ego made him plonk for the latter, and he'd had to duck his head to hide the smile of satisfaction.

Always possible, of course, that she was simply talking about the fact that he'd been making a hideous racket overhead for most of the past two days.

In fact, that was the most likely. It had been hard to miss.

His smile faded, and with a quiet sigh he put his ego back in the box and set about demolishing the quiche.

She was busy on the other side of the kitchen, working with swift efficiency born of long years of practice, and he watched her in silence as he ate.

She was still beautiful, her body perhaps a little thinner but softly rounded where it mattered. She could do with putting a little weight on, but if he was guilty of forgetting to eat, he was certain she was, too. Either that or she was often too busy to stop.

There was a clatter at the door, and it swung open, only the coats on the back stopping it from banging against the wall.

'Hi, Mum—oh. Hello. Who are you?'

He felt his palms break out, his heart pick up, and he pushed away his plate and stood up slowly.

'I'm Michael—and you must be Stephen. It's good to meet you—I've heard a lot about you.'

And extending his arm, he waited, his breath jammed in his throat, until Stephen reached out and, for the first time in his eight and a bit years, he placed his hand trustingly in his father's.

Emotion locked his throat solid. Dear God, he thought. He's the spitting image of me at that age. He's got my eyes. She'll see it—notice it instantly when we're side by side.

But she didn't.

She wiped her hands and turned, hugged her son, caught his coat before it slid off the table to the floor and hung it on the back of the door.

'So how was chess club?' she asked him, and he sighed, his face glum.

'Useless. I can't play. Dad was going to teach me some moves, but—'

He shrugged expressively, and Michael's heart contracted. Poor little tyke. Obviously Annie wasn't the only one to miss Roger. There was more to being a father than biology. The acknowledgement was curiously painful.

'Never mind,' she was saying, squeezing his shoulder comfortingly. 'Perhaps we can get a book from the library?'

'I could teach you,' he found himself saying in a strangled voice. He cleared his throat. 'If your mother doesn't mind?'

He looked into her eyes, saw the relief in them and felt the tension ease.

'Could you? Do you have time? You're so busy—'

'Not too busy to do that.' Never too busy for my son.

'Well, that would be wonderful. Thank you. We'll have to arrange a time.'

'We could do it now!' Stephen said, brightening, but she shook her head.

'No. You've got school tomorrow and it's already eight. You need to have a bath and get to bed. Have you had enough to eat?'

He nodded, and she kissed him and sent him upstairs to run his bath.

Michael tucked his chair under the table, feeling for his car keys in the pocket of his jeans, suddenly needing air. 'I should be off—leave you to get on,' he said, and he wasn't sure but there might have been a flicker of disappointment on her face.

Or maybe he was clutching at straws.

'Have you had enough to eat? There's more, if you're still hungry—'

'Absolutely not,' he said, summoning a smile. Any more food would have choked him, but that was nothing to do with the food and everything to do with her and his son and the emotion jamming his throat. 'Thank you, that was lovely, but I really ought to be going.'

'I'm just going to have a cup of tea—stay,' she said. 'We could talk about this chess thing.'

He shook his head. 'Another time,' he said. 'I could do with a bath myself, and a reasonably early night. I'll see you tomorrow.'

When I've had time to let all this sink in, and get over the feel of my son's hand in mine.

He looked down at her, standing so close that if he reached out he could reel her in against his chest and kiss her soft, full mouth until she whimpered. He backed away. No. Not yet. It was far, far too soon.

Thanking her again for the meal, he said goodnight, let himself out and drove slowly home, lost in thought.

'D'you think he'll really teach me to play chess?'

Annie smoothed her son's hair back off his brow and hugged him. 'I don't know. He said so, but he's busy.'

'Daddy said he'd teach me, but he died.'

'I know. I'm sorry. I know he would much rather have been here with us teaching you to play chess, but we don't always get what we want, and sometimes it's very hard.'

'I miss him,' Stephen mumbled, and Annie sighed.

'I know. I miss him, too.'

'Michael's nice.'

She tweaked his nose. 'Only because he said he'd teach you chess,' she said with a slightly breathless laugh, and tried not to think about Michael. She was thinking about him altogether too much as it was.

'What happened to his face?'

She hesitated. 'I'm not sure. I think he's probably had an accident. It's not the sort of thing you can ask.'

Stephen wrinkled his nose. 'It makes him look kind of funny. His mouth's a bit crooked.'

Like his sense of humour, she nearly said, but that was odd, because surely she didn't know anything about his sense of humour. Not really, not after so short a time. She was just imagining it, filling in the blanks, which was something she really had to stop doing, because she was getting more and more drawn to him, and it was crazy.

She'd done this with Etienne, and look where that had got her. Perhaps it was the way he had of focusing on her that Etienne had had, making her feel special. Important. The centre of his world.

But he wasn't Etienne, and she wasn't the girl she'd been nine years ago.

'Time to put your light out and go to sleep,' she said, kissing her son's cheek and snuggling the quilt around his skinny little shoulders. 'I'll see you in the morning. Night-night.'

'Sleep tight,' he mumbled back, dropping off already, and as she reached the door, he added, 'Ask him about the chess tomorrow.'

'OK. Now go to sleep. Love you.'

She went back downstairs, wondering if it was such a good idea getting Michael involved in Stephen's life. Mainly, she realised, because it meant involving him in hers, and hers, frankly, was involved enough!

It didn't stop him being the last thing she thought about as she fell asleep, though—and the first thing she thought about in the morning...

CHAPTER FOUR

HE FELT as if he'd been hit by a truck.

Carefully, gingerly, he rolled over and flexed his shoulders. Ouch. Not good.

He tried to sit up, and bit back a groan of pain and frustration.

That darned kitchen was out to get him—either that or the tension of the past few days had screwed him up. Both, probably. He tried again, fighting off the wave of nausea as he padded barefoot to the kitchen, fumbled pills out of the packet and propped his forehead against the front of the fridge while he waited for the glass to fill from the iced water dispenser.

The icy draught slid down his throat, reviving him as he swallowed the pills that hopefully would head this thing off before it turned into a full-blown migraine.

If he got lucky.

He opened his mouth, waggled his jaw experimentally and gave up. Damn. He needed to see Pete and get this mess sorted out.

The clock said eight-thirty. Annie would be in the tearoom—expecting him? He slumped at the kitchen table and knotted his fists together, then forced himself to relax. He wasn't going to get anywhere with this headache if he didn't let the tension go.

He sat back, rolled his shoulders and winced.

Maybe let the pills work.

Back to bed for a while—and try not to think about Annie.

It didn't work. He lay there, thinking about her quicksilver smile and the sparkle in her eyes, the freckles that dusted her nose and how good those soft, full lips would feel under his.

At least, under the areas of them that still had sensation.

'Oh, hell—'

He threw off the bedclothes, ignoring the screaming in his head, turned on the shower good and hot and propped himself up under the pounding spray. Half an hour later he was more relaxed, his head had eased with the tension in his shoulders and he felt halfway to being human again.

Now all he had to do was go over to the Ancient House and pretend to be doing something useful there. If nothing else, he ought to set a time for Stephen's chess lessons. The last thing he was going to do was let his son down, and no mere headache was going to get in the way.

Although only a total masochist would describe this demon in his skull as a mere headache. He phoned the osteopath before he left the house, got himself on the waiting list for an urgent appointment, and then he set off for the village. Perhaps he'd feel more human after a huge mug of Annie's coffee.

Or just her smile…

'You look rough.'

The cock-eyed grin he shot her did that thing to her insides again. 'Well, cheers. I feel much better for knowing that.'

'Heavy night?' she asked, and one brow climbed up towards his hairline.

'Are you always this sympathetic?'

'You think you deserve it, with a hangover?' she teased, but he shook his head and winced.

'No hangover,' he muttered, and she looked at him more

closely and felt a pang of guilt. A little frown pleated her brow.

'Michael, are you OK?'

'I've been better but I'll live. Don't worry, I won't keel over on the premises and compromise your reputation.'

She felt a bigger pang of guilt, and then a flutter of panic. Her reputation? 'It wasn't—you didn't get ill after the quiche, did you?'

He smiled ruefully. 'It's nothing to do with the quiche. You haven't poisoned me, you're safe. I get headaches. It's nothing.'

She frowned again. 'It doesn't look like nothing. Sit down before you fall down. What can I get you?'

'A quiet corner away from your piranhas,' he said with a slow smile, and she gave a little huff of laughter.

'I'll tell them you said that.'

'Please don't bother. A large filter coffee would be lovely. And we need to talk about this bill—'

'Don't be stupid. I've told you about that.'

He sighed and gave her a thoughtful look. 'Is this anything to do with why you struggle to make ends meet?' he murmured. 'Just how many freeloaders *do* you have, Annie?'

She felt herself colouring. 'I don't like to think of them as freeloaders—'

'So, several, then?'

'They're friends.'

'All of them?' he said softly, and she felt her defences crumble.

Her breath eased out on a sigh, and she shrugged. 'OK. You've got me. I'm soft. But it's my choice—'

'Of course it is. You'd mother the whole world, given half a chance, wouldn't you? Mother Teresa and Mrs Beeton rolled into one.'

She turned away, unwilling to discuss this with him. He sounded altogether too damn *right*. And if he didn't want her mothering him, fine. She wouldn't. She was all done mothering people anyway. She'd looked after Liz until she died, then she'd looked after Roger and the girls and Stephen—and all the time the tearoom had demanded attention—was *still* demanding attention. Half the people that came in were lame ducks.

He was right. Sickeningly. She mothered everybody. Well, not any more. She was Stephen's mother, and that was it. The rest of them were off her list. Starting with him. He, of all of them, could afford it.

She turned back with his coffee in her hand and met his eyes defiantly. 'That'll be one pound fifty,' she said, thrusting it at him, and his eyes crinkled with a smile.

'Better,' he murmured, and taking the coffee from her hand, he dropped the change into her palm and headed for the little table at the back, the one she'd have to lose if she got access to the garden.

It wouldn't be much of a loss, she thought. Nobody liked sitting there; it was too much in the way for people going to the loo. But Michael sat himself down at it, turning his back to the window and watching her thoughtfully over his cup, and she realised for the first time that it had a clear view of her working in the kitchen area and he was taking full advantage of it.

Hmph. Perhaps she *should* get rid of that table. Right now. Immediately.

She turned back to the mess, quickly emptying and reloading the dishwasher and setting it off again in an attempt to tame the chaos. It had been hell first thing, a coach party *en route* to the coast pausing for an early coffee hard on the heels of the breakfast crowd. She hadn't had a minute to draw breath, and if she didn't get ahead while she had the chance—

'Hiya!'

She gave an inward groan. Grace and Jackie. Just what she needed.

'Hi,' she said, dredging up a smile.

'Well, don't look so pleased to see us. What's the matter, no Michael today?'

'He's here—over there, by the back window,' she pointed out. 'Leave him alone, he's got a headache.'

'Oh, poor baby,' Grace murmured, and immediately headed over to him. 'Hi. How's the head?'

'Improving.'

'Want some company? You're welcome to join us.'

His grin was fleeting. 'I'm OK. I'm off in a minute, anyway,' he told her, and Annie felt a stupid sense of loss. Crazy. She was letting herself get far too involved with this man—

'So, it's just us, kiddo,' Grace said, coming back to the counter and grinning at Jackie and Annie. 'What shall we have, Jack? Something messy and complicated, like a bacon sandwich and a latte?'

'Or you could just have a scone and filter coffee and keep out of my hair until I've got the place straight,' she found herself saying.

Their jaws all but dropped. 'Are you OK?'

'Just busy. Don't worry. I'll do you a bacon sandwich—'

'No—no. Don't. A scone's fine. I'll have cheese.'

'I'll have fruit. And filter coffee's fine. No rush. Thanks.'

They scuttled over to the big window table at the front and slid on to the chairs, watching her warily, and she gave an inward sigh and took their coffees over. Lattes, as usual, to assuage her guilt.

'I'm sorry. I'm being a bitch.'

'What's the matter?'

She looked at Jackie and shrugged. 'I don't know. I feel—unsettled. I just had words with Michael.'

'Words?'

And of course these were the last people she could tell, since they, largely, were the subject of the argument.

'I was sticking my nose in,' he explained, approaching so silently she hadn't heard him. 'Annie, I'm sorry, you're right, it's none of my business. I'll see you later. I've just had a call from the osteopath. I'm going to get my head fixed. Maybe I'll get my diplomacy back as a side effect, you never know.'

'Want to get me some?' she suggested, sending him a silent apology with her eyes, and he smiled slowly and leant over and dropped a kiss on her cheek.

Just like that. Out of nowhere.

'You'll do. I'll see you later,' he murmured, and went out, leaving Jackie and Grace open-mouthed and her legs on the point of collapsing.

Jackie shut her mouth, opened it again and whispered, 'Wow.'

Grace just shook her head and sighed lustily. 'I smell romance in the air.'

'Rubbish,' Annie said briskly, scooting back into the kitchen and wondering just exactly how high her colour was. 'Two scones coming up.' And no doubt a whole heap of personal and highly intrusive questions!

'Better?'

He nodded slowly. 'Much. I think it was wrestling with the kitchen. I'm OK now, but I could do with a quiet few days. I might devote myself to planning. Had any more thoughts about down here?'

She sighed and shook her head. 'Sorry, no. I haven't had time—and anyway, I can't afford to do anything to it—'

'I thought we'd dealt with that.'

She met his eyes squarely. 'Now who's mothering?'

A glimmer of appreciation flared briefly in those gorgeous blue depths. 'It *is* my property. I'm entitled to improve it if I want to. And I do.'

'And I still don't know why.'

He shrugged. 'Maybe because I'm a perfectionist and I don't like to see things not working as they should.'

'Such as?' she retorted, starting to bristle again.

He shrugged again. 'The store room?'

OK. She had to give him that. The store was woefully inadequate.

'And the kitchen area. It really isn't very well organised. You could have much more storage here—'

'I can't afford it,' she said again, patiently, as if she were talking to an idiot.

It wasn't lost on him. He grinned and shook his head.

'We have dealt with this,' he repeated, just as patiently, and stood his ground, arms folded, looking solid and immoveable and for all the world like a battle-scarred warrior who'd ended up in her tearoom by mistake.

She wasn't going to win.

She chucked the tea towel she was torturing into the bag in the corner and he arched a brow quizzically.

'Throwing in the towel?' he murmured, and she shot him a saccharine smile.

'Very clever. I haven't got time to argue.'

'Good,' he said, his smile widening, and she ground her teeth.

'So much for the return of your diplomacy,' she bit out, and he chuckled. Damn him, he actually laughed at her! A couple entered the tearoom behind him, and grabbing her order pad like a lifeline, she muttered, 'Excuse me,' squeezed past him and tried very hard to ignore the tingle running through her from that fleeting encounter with his lean, hard body.

Impossible. Heat zinged through her, and she couldn't have been more aware of him if he'd been wired up to the National Grid. The wretched man was going to be the death of her!

She wrote down their order and went back behind the counter, shooting him a wary look. 'You still here?'

'I was hoping for a pot of tea, a scone and a few minutes of your time. If that's possible.'

He looked patient, long-suffering and perhaps a little disappointed in her. She bit her lip, took a deep breath and dredged up a smile. 'I'm sorry. I'm behaving like a child. I don't even know what we're fighting about.'

'You're just not used to people doing anything but taking,' he said quietly. 'Well, I've got news for you, Annie. I don't want to take anything from you—nothing at all.'

And he turned on his heel and walked out.

Good Lord! He'd been on the point of telling her just how much he wanted to give her. Starting with his soul!

Idiot. He opened the door to the flat, walked slowly and heavily upstairs and sat down in the wreckage of the kitchen. Well, at least it was clear now. He propped himself against the wall and studied it dispiritedly.

Why the hell were they fighting? They hadn't fought before—not for a moment! They'd teased and laughed and flirted—

And he hadn't been her landlord, and he'd been playing a totally different person, a charming womaniser who'd set about disarming her from the first meeting.

Now they were both different, he because he was actually being himself, and she because she was older, wiser, laden with responsibility and rushed off her feet. And he kept hounding her to make changes when she'd had so many she probably never wanted to change anything ever again!

'Fool,' he muttered, crossing his arms on his knees and resting his aching head on them. He ought to go home to bed, but he couldn't leave it like this—

'Michael?'

He lifted his head and studied her thoughtfully. 'Hi. Have you escaped?'

She laughed, a soft, rueful little ripple of sound that brought a lump to his throat.

'For a moment. Jude's minding the shop.' She came and sat down beside him on the dusty floor, avoiding his eyes. 'Look, I'm really sorry. I don't know what's going on. Can we start today again?'

He reached out a hand, and after a moment's hesitation she put hers in it.

'Truce?' she murmured, and he smiled at her, tugged her gently towards him and dropped a kiss on her startled lips.

'Oh!' she said, her soft voice breathless, and then she smiled, looking suddenly young and innocent and twenty-one again, and his gut clenched.

'I take it that's a yes?' she said, and he smiled.

'That's a yes,' he said, his voice gruff, and pulling her back again, he kissed her once more, then let her go quickly, before he could do anything else stupid to screw this up. He got to his feet, held out his hand and helped her up, then dropped her hand fast before he got too darned used to holding it.

'I don't suppose you want to come back down and have that chat?' she said, meeting his eyes with a certain hesitation.

The smile wouldn't be held back. 'What—rather than sit here on a cold, dusty floor and stare at this lot? I think I could be talked into it.' He held a hand out towards the door. 'After you.'

She turned away from him with a smile, and he saw the back of her trousers.

'Oops. Dust,' he told her, jerking his head slightly in the direction of her delectable bottom. She peered over her shoulder, brushed ineffectually at her seat and then looked up at him.

'That better?'

'Marginally. Here, let me.' And, without allowing himself to think about it, he took his hand and swiped it firmly over her taut, trim backside. 'That's got it,' he said, swallowing hard, and ramming his hand in his pocket where it couldn't get into any more mischief, he followed her downstairs.

'So—tea and a scone, was it?' she asked, and he gave a slightly distracted smile and nodded.

'Please.' He tilted his head slightly towards Jude. 'So—who did you say that was?'

'Judy—my assistant. She helps me out on Wednesdays so I can go and cook, but we've been so busy today I was going to stay and help her clear up.'

'So you don't really have time to talk?'

She looked at her watch, feeling the pressure of all the things she still had to do before Stephen finished school. 'I could later more easily—after I shut? About five-thirty? That would be better.'

He nodded. 'I'll come back then. What about Stephen?'

'He comes here from school. He'll be here about a quarter to four. He's OK, he sits at the table and does his homework if I'm not at home. He'll be fine.'

'Right. I'll see you later.'

She watched him go, her bottom still tingling from the touch of his hand, and she lifted her hand and traced her lips, still dazed.

'You OK?'

'I'm fine, Jude.' She looked around, seeing the place suddenly almost empty. Typical, just when she'd sent him off. 'Look, I tell you what, why don't I go home and throw together some more pasta bakes? And we'll need scones for tomorrow. Anything else you've noticed?'

'We're low on apple cake. I've just sold the last two bits that were out, and there's only a couple in the tin.'

'OK. I'll do some of that if I've got time. Can you send Stephen over when he arrives, and I'll come and lock up at five-thirty. If Michael comes back before I do, can you give him a coffee and ask him to hang on?'

'Sure.'

She ignored the curiosity in her assistant's eyes, grabbed what she needed to take home and headed out of the door before something else cropped up. It always did.

She was up to her arms in flour when Stephen wandered in, munching an apricot slice. 'Judy gave it to me,' he said by way of explanation, and she nodded and dropped a fleeting kiss on his head.

Fleeting because he ducked the moment he sensed her coming, and shot under her arm and out of the room. 'I'm going to the loo,' he said, vanishing up the stairs.

'Don't be long, you've got homework to do,' she called after him. She knew quite well what he'd be doing—sitting in there with his nose in a book, hiding from his homework behind the locked door. She sighed. Oh, well, at least it kept him out of her hair while she was cooking, and he could always do his homework while Michael was here.

In fact, that would be better, she decided, and left Stephen to it.

'So how's it going?'

Michael raked up a smile from somewhere. 'Oh, up and down. We had a bit of a fight today.'

Ruth raised an eyebrow and settled herself more comfortably on his sofa. 'About?'

He shrugged. 'Nothing, really. She has this bunch of freeloaders—'

'Her support group. Yeah, I know. Grace and Jackie and Chris.'

'Amongst others.'

'So don't tell me—you called them freeloaders?'

He shrugged again. 'And if I did?'

Ruth rolled her eyes. 'They're her friends, Michael. She loves them to bits, and they love her. She needs them.'

'But they could still pay—'

'They do pay. They just pay less. They don't really cost her anything, they just don't make her a profit. That's allowed, isn't it? Not to make a profit from your friends?'

Suddenly he started to see it from Annie's side, and with a groan he dropped back against the sofa and rolled his head towards her. 'Do you have to be right about everything?' he said wryly.

'Only if you insist on being wrong.'

He laughed. 'So how's life with Tim?'

'Wonderful.' She turned, wriggling round so she was facing him, and gave him a searching look. 'So—I take it she still doesn't know who you are?'

He shook his head. 'No. Not yet. But I'm getting there.'

'And does she like you?'

He thought of the kiss, and the startled, pleased expression on her face, and felt himself colour slightly. 'I think so. I hope so. It's not as easy this time.'

'That's because you're being you, and you're a miserable, grumpy old sod most of the time.'

'Well, cheers,' he grunted. 'With friends like you—'

'Someone needs to keep you aware of reality,' she said drily. 'So when are you going to tell her?'

He shrugged. 'I don't know. Not yet. It's so complicated.'

She worried her lip with her teeth. 'Be careful, Michael. Don't leave it too long. I know your reasons, and I respect them, but you have to see it from her side.'

He nodded. 'I know. I won't muck about. Just as soon as I feel we've got a chance, I'll tell her.'

'You mind you do. What about Stephen?'

He felt his face soften, and looked away. 'He's a great kid. I met him last night.'

'He's lovely, isn't he? Bit of a handful.'

'Is he? Odd, he didn't seem it.'

'She's brought him up very well. They always insisted on manners, so you would have seen the good side of him, but there's a stubborn streak in there a mile wide.'

'I wonder which one of us he gets that from?' he murmured with a grin.

'Either,' Ruth said bluntly. 'There's nothing to choose between you. So when are you seeing them again?'

'This evening—five-thirty. And I'm going to give him chess lessons.'

Ruth nodded. 'Nice one. He'll like that. Roger started teaching him just before he died.'

'I gather.'

'Just don't leave it too long,' she said again, and with a little wave of her hand, she left him there, thinking about what she'd said about seeing it from Annie's side.

She'd understand—wouldn't she? After all, what choice did he have? If he just walked right up to her and said, Hi, remember me, you used to call me Etienne and for the last nine years you've thought I was dead, but now I'm back, looking mangled and unrecognisable and nothing like that warm, charismatic guy you fell for, and I want you to marry me and let me share my life with you and your son, he could just see how well that would go down!

And because of the Mother Teresa/Mrs Beeton thing, she'd take him straight back into her life, regardless of her personal feelings, and he'd never know if she'd married him for Stephen's sake or because she loved him.

And there was no way he was letting her throw away her chances of happiness on a loveless marriage.

Even if it was with him.

CHAPTER FIVE

'ANNIE not here?'

Judy looked up and shook her head at him. 'She's gone home to bake. She'll be back at five-thirty to close.'

He nodded. 'OK. I'll go over there. Thanks.'

He crossed the corner of the square, walked up to her front door and rang the bell. He heard a yell and the thunder of feet on stairs, then the door was yanked back on its hinges and Stephen stood there grinning at him.

'Hi. Have you come to teach me chess?' he asked without preamble, and Michael felt his lips twitch.

'Maybe. Depends what your mother says. Do you have homework?'

He picked up the sound of her footsteps approaching, then she appeared through a doorway, a welcoming smile on her face.

'Hi. I wondered if you'd come over. Come on through. I'm up to my eyes.'

Up to her elbows, certainly. He followed her to the kitchen, taking in all the little period details of the house as he went—the pictures on the walls, the antique furniture, the lovely tiles on the hall floor, the smooth curl on the end of the banister rail—it was elegant and welcoming, yet somehow—stifling. Steeped in the nineteenth century and up to its neck in tradition. Not her at all.

Unlike the kitchen, which was all Annie. Clutter was strewn from end to end—wire cooling trays and pots and pans and the air rich with the scent of cinnamon and apples, coming from a huge shallow pan of what looked like her Dutch apple cake.

It was fast becoming one of his favourites and, without asking him, she cut a slice out of the corner of the tray and slid the plate towards him on the table.

'Here. It's still warm. I'll make tea—do you want cream with that, by the way?'

'No, thanks, it's fine like this, and tea will be lovely. What about Stephen?'

'Yuck, I hate apple cake,' he said with feeling. 'Can I have a scone?'

'No, you've already had an apricot slice since you got home. You won't want your supper.'

'But I'm *starving*!' he said with all the pathos of the young, and Michael had to look away to hide the smile.

'Have you done your homework?' she asked, and he sighed heavily.

'Sort of.'

'Is it finished?'

'Sort of.'

'That would be a no, then. Go and do it now, please, before supper.'

'But Michael was going to teach me to play chess!'

'No, Michael was going to ask your mother if and when it would be all right,' Michael corrected, and earned himself a Brownie point.

'Homework first,' she said firmly, and he flounced out with a sigh and banged the door just the teeniest bit behind him.

'Little monster,' she muttered.

'He's just checking me out and testing you.'

She rolled her eyes. 'Tell me about it. I think bringing him up's going to be a handful. He can be a nightmare.' She set a pot of tea down on the table, looked at him thoughtfully and said, 'So what was it you wanted to talk about?'

He shrugged and smiled. Another wry, awry effort because he could see how busy she was and all he'd really wanted was her company.

So he lied. Again.

'It was about the chess, really,' he said, and she looked at him in puzzlement.

'Oh. I'd wondered—'

She broke off, looking confused, and suddenly he didn't want to lie. He wanted her to know the truth—and he wanted to know what she wondered. So he asked her.

And she sighed. 'I don't know. Nothing. It's silly.'

'What?'

She shrugged. 'Nothing. I'm being ridiculous.'

She turned back to the stove, and he stood up and went over to her, cupping her shoulders lightly in his hands and making her jump.

'Oh! You startled me. I didn't hear you—'

'What did you think?' he asked softly. 'That I wanted to spend time with you?'

She turned in his hands, looking up at him with wide, puzzled eyes. 'Is that true?'

He nodded. 'Yes. The chess was just an excuse. I promised him I'd teach him, and I will. I'd like to. But that's not why I wanted to see you. Why I want to see you.'

He could see a pulse beating in her throat, deep in the warm, soft hollow at its base. He had an urge to touch it, to lower his head and stroke his tongue lightly over it, to feel it beat against his flesh—

'All finished!'

She sucked in a huge breath and stepped back, colliding with the stove, her eyes wide and shocked, her pupils flared.

And he hadn't even touched her, except the lightest touch of his hands on her shoulders.

God alone knows what would happen when he did. It would be like a match to tinder. He stepped back, dropping his hands and sucking in a deep, steadying breath of his own before he turned to his son.

'Are you sure?' he asked. 'I don't want to be responsible for you messing up at school because we're playing chess when you should be working.'

'I have done it, I promise,' he said, meeting Michael's eyes squarely without a trace of evasion.

Either he was as good a liar as his father or he was telling the truth.

Michael gave him the benefit of the doubt. 'OK. Have you got a chess set?'

He nodded and ran out, then ran back. 'Where is it?'

'In your dad's study, on the bottom shelf on the left, I think,' Annie said. 'The red box.'

He reappeared a minute later with a faded red box, opened the lid and started to extract the pieces and set them up on the board.

'Well, you're doing that right, so you must know something,' Michael said with a smile, and Stephen grinned back.

'I'm not that useless!' he said, and over his head Michael saw Annie roll her eyes and smile.

'I have to go and shut up the tearoom. Are you OK if I leave you two together for a moment?'

He met her eyes. 'Of course. Take as long as you need. We'll be fine, won't we, Sport?'

'Yeah, we're fine.'

They exchanged grins, and something inside Michael's

chest tightened up and squeezed, so that he could hardly breathe or swallow.

'Right,' he said, clearing his throat. 'You're the youngest, you start.'

By the time Annie came back, they were halfway through the game, and even she could see that Stephen was struggling. Oh, dear. She'd rather hoped Michael would give him a chance, but maybe next time—

'You can't do that, you'll put yourself in check.'

'How—oh. OK.'

Oh, dear, he sounded so crestfallen.

'I'm not going to win, am I?' he said soulfully, and Michael shook his head.

'Sorry, son. Not this time.'

Son. Oh, God, if only. Stephen so badly needed a father— and not an invalid as Roger had become, but a vital, healthy, active man who could keep up with his antics and stay one step ahead of that busy and inquisitive little mind—

And she was getting ahead of herself, talking of staying one step ahead. Try ten. Three days, Annie, and you've got him playing father to your son.

'Checkmate.'

'What? Oh, no! I didn't see that coming!'

Stephen folded his arms and threw himself back in the chair, a pout on his lips his sisters would have been proud of.

'You'll get there. You just need time. Set them up again. I'll teach you some moves, help you think it through, now I know how your mind works.'

Annie stifled a laugh at that, and Michael lifted his head and met her eyes. His lips twitched, and she had to turn away, biting her own lip to stop the chuckle from escaping.

'What do you fancy for supper, guys?' she asked, and Stephen promptly told her lasagne. No surprises there, then.

'What about you, Michael?'

'Am I staying?' he asked, and she turned back and met his eyes.

'If you like,' she said, not wanting to seem too pushy, too—well, too needy, really. 'I mean, I expect you're busy, but if you're not, there's plenty—'

'I'm not busy,' he said, and she ground to a halt and smiled.

'Good. Lasagne all right with you?'

'Whatever. I'm not fussy. You know me, I'll eat anything so long as I don't have to cook it.'

So she sliced a good three portions from the fresh pan of lasagne she'd made earlier, put them into the oven to heat and turned her attention to the salad.

'Do I *have* to have salad?' Stephen said in his best long-suffering voice, as if he was force-fed it three times a day.

'Yes, you do,' she replied. 'It's good for you.'

'Don't care. Hate it.'

'You don't hate it—and don't be rude, please, or you'll be putting that chess set away instantly.'

He stifled a sigh and turned his attention back to the game. 'OK,' he said heavily. 'I'll eat salad. Michael, could you show me how to win?'

Michael's lips twitched again.

'I think we need to start a little further back. How about some opening moves?'

She watched them as she prepared their supper and cleared up the chaos from the afternoon's cooking fest. He was good with Stephen, she realised. Very good. Patient, explaining things carefully without patronising him, but pitching it just right to stretch him a little and not so much that he gave up.

And then he called a halt, just when she was about to, and she realised he'd been keeping an eye on her, too, and checking her progress so he could be the one to stop the lesson.

So she wasn't always the nag, the scold, the one wielding the big stick.

And she found she was suddenly hugely grateful to him, because being a single parent was difficult and endless and sharing it, even in this small way, truly lightened the load.

Supper was different as well. More fun. She and Stephen often had fun then, talking over silly things that had happened in the day, but with Michael there it was—well, it was more interesting.

And when Stephen had gone up to bed and she'd finished bagging up her pasta bakes in their individual dishes and put them in the freezer outside in the garage, they'd sat down together in the little sitting room at the back and shared a pot of tea in a companionable silence.

Then Michael looked at his watch and sighed, getting to his feet. 'I ought to go. I've got things to do, a couple of phone calls to make.'

She nodded, getting up to see him out. 'Of course you have. I'm sorry, I've kept you too long—'

'No, you haven't. You've been lovely.'

'Not a cross between Mother Teresa and Mrs Beeton?' she teased with only a flicker of hurt, and he clicked his tongue and shook his head and pulled her gently into his arms.

'I'm sorry,' he murmured into her hair.

'Don't be. You were right. I collect lame ducks. Always have. It makes a change to have someone to lean on.'

He squeezed her gently. 'What I said—about not wanting anything from you,' he said quietly. 'It wasn't quite the truth. What I meant was, I don't want to take anything you aren't ready to give me. I didn't mean I didn't want you.'

She looked up, her breath catching at the gruff, husky

note in his voice, and her eyes met his and locked. Good grief. She thought she'd burn up with the need in them, but then suddenly it was gone, as suddenly as it had come, and she wondered if she'd imagined it.

He lifted his hand, grazing his knuckles gently over her cheek. 'Goodnight, Annie,' he murmured, and lowering his head, he brushed his lips lightly, tentatively, over hers.

'Goodnight, Michael,' she whispered, and lifting herself up on tiptoe, she kissed him back.

For a moment he stiffened, but then he gave a rough, tattered groan and slanted his mouth more securely over hers and kissed her as if he was dying for her.

Dear God.

It only lasted seconds. Maybe four, five? And then he wrenched himself away and dropped his hands from her shoulders as if she might burn him. He could very well be right—

'Sleep tight. I'll see you tomorrow,' he said, and all but bolted for the door.

She watched him go, then locked up, went back into the kitchen and fed the cat, made another cup of tea and settled down again on the sofa to think about the feel of his lips and the heat of his mouth and the need in his eyes.

Sleep tight?

She didn't sleep a wink.

He avoided her on Thursday. He had to. Things were moving far too fast.

What the hell had he been *thinking* about to kiss her like that?

'Too much, you fool,' he muttered, wrenching the bath away from the wall without even thinking about what it was doing to his neck. To hell with his neck. He didn't care about his neck. All he cared about was Annie, and kissing her again, and—

'Damn!'

The blood spurted from the cut, and he glared at it in disgust. He'd have to wash it.

Except, of course, he'd taken out the basin already, and the only running water was in the loo. Not a great idea.

Which left him no choice but to go back downstairs and use the basin in Annie's cloakroom to sort it out. And that meant seeing Annie.

Well, his mind might think that was a lousy idea, but his body was all for it. With a grunt of disgust he tugged his rugby shirt down to give him greater privacy and ran down the stairs, his finger clutched in a wad of loo paper.

'Oops,' she said with a knowing grin. 'Want a plaster?'

'No. I think I need a nurse,' he muttered. A psychiatric one.

'I'll come,' she said, picking up the first aid kit and chivvying him through to the cloakroom.

The *tiny* cloakroom, with her pressed up against him clucking and tutting and pulling the cut open and pouring icy water into it—

'Ouch!'

'Baby,' she teased. 'You'll live. It needs to be clean.'

'I'm sure it is now,' he said drily, and handed her another handful of loo roll to dry it.

She stuck a plaster neatly over the cut, told him to apply pressure to it and cleaned up the basin.

'Sorry about the mess,' he said, but she just threw him a smile that made his body shriek with delight and patted his cheek.

'Don't worry. Although I'm going to have to restock my first aid kit at this rate.'

'I'll buy you a new one,' he promised. 'I'll get myself

one while I'm at it. Or perhaps a job lot. Wonder if I'll get a bulk discount?'

He was just talking for the sake of it, but she chuckled and shooed him back out, went behind the counter and reached for a teapot.

'Tea? Or are you still on coffee?'

'Tea would be lovely,' he said, giving up on the idea of going back upstairs without a qualm.

Moments later she set the pot down on the table, followed by two cups, a milk jug and a slice of apple cake. 'Here. I expect you need this,' she said, sliding on to the chair beside his and pushing the cake towards him.

'I do. I missed lunch,' he said unnecessarily, and met her eyes.

Only for a second, though, before hers skittered away.

'Um—about last night,' she began, and he sighed.

'I know. I'm sorry. I was out of line—'

'*You* were?' she exclaimed, then lowered her voice hastily. 'No. It was me. I kissed you back. You just gave me a peck, and I—' She floundered to a halt, and he found himself holding his breath.

'You—what?' he coaxed, desperate to hear what she was going to say.

'I pushed it,' she confessed hurriedly. 'Turned it into something it wasn't meant to be.'

'I didn't exactly object,' he pointed out, thinking he ought to be fair about that, at least, and it got a chuckle from her.

'No—I suppose you didn't, but it wasn't fair to move the goalposts. There you were, just being polite—'

'Polite?' he mouthed, and gave a strangled little laugh. 'You think I was being *polite*?' He stuck a finger under her chin, steered her head round to face him and waited for her to meet his eyes. Finally.

'I was not being polite,' he said firmly. 'At all. Not even slightly.'

'Oh,' she said, and gave a relieved little laugh. 'I wondered if that was why you skipped lunch.'

He groaned. 'It was—in a way. I thought I'd overdone it. Pushed you.'

'Pushed *me*—oh, no. No, not at all. It was—fine.'

Fine? She thought his kiss was *fine*? He was obviously losing his touch.

'Um—Stephen said thanks for the chess lesson, by the way. It was all he could talk about at breakfast.'

He smiled. 'He's welcome. When do you want me to teach him again?'

She met his eyes then, searchingly, and he found the contact unnerving. God only knows what she'd see if she looked too hard. 'Are you sure it's OK?'

He forced a grin. 'I'll do anything for supper.'

And she relaxed, at last, and laughed softly.

'Tomorrow?'

'Sure. Same sort of time?'

She nodded. 'Well, no, actually, a bit later,' she amended. 'Come at six-thirty—that'll give me time to sort this lot out— oh, no, Stephen's at a friend's house. Saturday?'

He nodded. 'Sure.'

'Just come round the back and let yourself in. It's easier if I'm busy in the kitchen.'

He nodded again, then stabbed his fork into the apple cake and sliced off a chunk. She was right, he was starving—and not only for the cake. It made a good start, though.

'Hi, Honey, I'm home!' he sang, knocking on the back door as he opened it, and then he ground to a halt and shut his eyes, wincing inwardly with embarrassment.

Great. Just what he needed!

'Sorry,' he said, opening his eyes and greeting the two young women at the table with a sheepish grin. 'I didn't realise Annie had company. I'm Michael.'

He held out his hand, and they shook it in turn.

'I'm Kate,' the younger one said with a curious but friendly smile, 'and this is Vicky. We're her stepdaughters.'

'Ah,' he said, and nodded. 'Of course you are. I can see your father in you both. Um—is she around?'

'She's upstairs—she said something about sorting out the beds. She wasn't expecting us.'

He was on the point of telling them to go and make their own beds when he realised it was actually none of his business.

Kate was still looking at him curiously, but Vicky's look was altogether more searching. 'Are you in the habit of walking in like that?' she asked, her voice less than friendly, and Kate stared at her in obvious astonishment.

'Vicky!'

Vicky was no problem to him. He could deal with her with one hand tied behind his back. But, for the sake of harmony and because it was their house, too, he reined in his temper. 'No, I'm not, actually,' he told them. 'Annie told me to come in, though. I'm here to give Stephen a chess lesson.'

'Really?'

'Really,' he said drily, his grip on his temper slipping a fraction at her arch tone. 'Do you have a problem with that?'

'Only if you're using it as an excuse to get in her knickers.'

He froze, astonished at the unexpectedness of her attack and her choice of words, while Kate coloured furiously and hissed 'Vix!' at her sister in horror.

After a lengthy silence which he did nothing to alleviate, he leant towards Vicky, propped both hands on the table, and said very slowly and carefully, 'If I wanted to get into your stepmother's knickers—which, by the way, is absolutely none of your business—I wouldn't stoop to using her son as an excuse.'

And then he straightened up and went over to the hall door, just as it opened and Annie came in.

'Michael! I didn't hear you arrive. Have you met the girls?'

'Oh, yes,' he said softly, his back to them. 'I've already been warned off.'

'Really?' Her eyes widened, then narrowed. 'Well, we wouldn't want to give them the wrong idea,' she murmured and, going up on tiptoe, she hooked a hand around the back of his neck, pulled him down and kissed him.

It was just a peck, but it was proprietorial and it made him want to beat his chest like Tarzan.

She grinned at him, dropped back on to her heels and moved past him.

'So, have you put the kettle on for Michael, girls?' she said cheerfully, and Kate got up, still clearly flustered, and grabbed the kettle and shoved it under the tap.

Vicky was made of sterner stuff. She gave him a baleful look. 'I'll bring my things in from the car,' she said shortly, and disappeared.

'Stephen's in the study,' Annie told him. 'Why don't you go through and find him, and I'll bring you some tea in a moment?'

He nodded, having a fair idea of what was about to take place, and not wanting to be in Vicky's shoes for anything. 'Don't be too hard on her,' he murmured.

'Hard?' she said, and he realised she was quietly seething. 'I'll give her hard. Don't worry about Vicky. She'll get over it.'

'Annie—she loves you.'

And her eyes softened, and her shoulders dropped inches. 'OK. I won't kill her. This time.'

'Promise?'

She smiled up at him. 'I promise. Go on.'

He went, keeping one ear out for the screams and cries he felt sure would follow, but there were none. She appeared five minutes later with a cup of tea, set it down beside him, glanced at the chessboard and said, 'Oh. You seem to have lost a lot of pieces.'

'Mmm. He's a quick study.'

And Stephen grinned up at her, and he just hoped she had the sense not to say anything else.

'Come on, Sport, thrash me and get it over with,' he said with a sigh, and Stephen turned his attention back to the board and rubbed his hands together with glee.

'Checkmate,' he said with a grin a mile wide, and Michael leant over the corner of the desk, ruffled his son's hair and grinned right back.

'So. Who's going to tell me the truth?' she said, and Kate looked away.

Vicky sighed. 'He walked in, saying, "Hi, Honey, I'm home!" in a stupid voice. What was I supposed to think?'

She could just imagine his embarrassment and confusion when he'd seen the girls. It made her laugh just to picture it. 'Oh, dear,' she said after a moment. 'So you put two and two together, made about twenty-five and warned him off, is that right?'

'Is that what he told you?'

'That he'd been warned off? Yes.' She leant forwards

and covered Vicky's hand, squeezing it gently. 'Vix, he's my landlord. And he's a friend. And really, if I wanted to have a relationship with him, there isn't a good reason why I shouldn't, is there?'

She shook her head, looking embarrassed and unhappy. 'I'm sorry. It's just—'

'What?'

'Well, Dad.'

'Vicky, your father's dead, darling—and anyway, you know we didn't have that kind of a relationship. Your mother was the only woman in the world for him, and he'd be the last person to want me to sit about and mope.'

'I'm sorry,' she said again. 'It's just that he's so—'

'So what?' she prompted, when Vicky broke off.

'So—I don't know. Male! Macho. Dangerous.'

'Dangerous?' she exclaimed, laughed. 'Michael's not dangerous! He'd kill me with kindness if I let him. He keeps trying to get me to extend the tearoom and won't take any more rent—'

'Rent? Your *landlord*?' Kate squealed, cottoning on at last. 'He's Michael *Harding*?'

Vicky went pale. 'Oh, my God. I've just told one of the richest and most successful authors on the best-seller list to leave my stepmother alone. I can't believe it. Oh, God, I want to die.'

'I'm sure that won't be necessary,' Michael said gently, hooking out a chair and dropping into it beside her. 'Anyway, if it makes you feel better, your brother just thrashed me at chess.'

'Good grief, you must be crap,' Kate said with a stifled laugh, and he chuckled.

'Or just a very nice man,' Annie said, smiling at him. 'Don't let him win too often. He'll be insufferable.'

Michael snorted. 'Don't worry, I won't. My ego can't cope with it.'

And, getting to his feet, he headed back out, just a gentle squeeze on her shoulder to tell her—and the girls—that she wasn't forgotten while he was out of the room.

Their eyes met, and Vicky groaned.

'I'm going to have to apologise, aren't I?' she said.

'It might be nice. And while you're on a roll, I've put clean sheets out on your beds. You could make them up to save me a job. Kate, fancy helping me with the supper?'

'Sure.'

And that, she hoped, was the end of that.

CHAPTER SIX

'LOOK—I'm really sorry.'

Michael looked up at Vicky and his heart ached for her.

'It's OK, Vicky.'

'No. I shouldn't have said what I did. I can't believe I did—'

He gave a grunt of laughter. 'I had a moment's doubt, I must say. Followed by the urge to rip your head off, but what would that achieve? And then I sat down and thought about what you must be feeling—what you're going through at the moment, you and Kate, and it all made much more sense.'

She shook her head. 'It's not about Dad.'

'I know. It's about Annie, and what she means to you, and preserving the status quo. And suddenly a man appears in her life and the status quo is threatened. And my guess is you panicked, just like I did when my mother died. My father had been an invalid for years, and whether it was the strain of looking after him or just one of those crazy things, she got cancer.'

'Oh, God, I'm sorry. I know how that feels. How old were you?'

'Eighteen. She died when I was twenty, and he couldn't go on without her. By the time I was twenty-one I'd lost them both. I don't know if he died of a broken heart or because of his old injuries—he'd been a bomb disposal officer, and got caught in a chemical blast—but whatever, he only lasted months after she died, and I didn't know what the hell was going to happen to me.

'I was at university, the family home had to be packed up and sorted out, and without my godparents I think I would have lost it. As it was I joined the army and ended up in the SAS. Dangerous and messy and exactly what I needed, but my godparents were always there for me, like a safety net, in case it all went wrong. And they still are. And the fact that the house isn't there any more, and I can't just go home and go up to the bedroom I used as a child, somehow doesn't matter. I've got my own life now, as you will, and just because Annie needs to move on with her life doesn't mean she won't be there for you, just as my godparents are there for me. She loves you to bits, you know. Nothing's going to change that.'

Her eyes were sparkling, filling with tears, and as he watched one welled over and slid down her cheek.

'I just miss them both. I don't think I'll ever get over losing Mum. I was only twelve. You shouldn't lose your Mum when you're twelve. And then when Dad died last year—it wasn't exactly a surprise, you know, but—' She broke off, shrugged, and he reached out a hand and squeezed her shoulder gently.

'I know. It's always a shock. Even when you know, even when you're expecting it, there's always that last breath, and then they're gone. And that's never going to be easy to accept, even when you can see a mile off that it's coming.'

She nodded, another tear joining the first, and she brushed them away impatiently. 'Kate seems to be taking it so much better.'

'Perhaps because she doesn't feel any responsibility? I mean, if Annie gets married again—'

Her head snapped up. 'Are you going to marry her?'

He laughed, wondering if it sounded as strained as it felt. 'Good grief, she only met me on Monday. I think that's a little hasty, even by my standards. I was just hypothesising. So, if she were to get married again, what next? Kate would assume you'd sort it. Wherever you are would become her home, her focus, unless Annie's new husband was prepared to welcome you into his home.'

Vicky chewed her lip worriedly. 'And if not? What would happen to this house?'

He shrugged. 'I don't know. It's something you'd have to discuss with Annie if it ever arose. But I can't imagine her making a new life that excluded you; she's not that sort of woman. I think she'd give up her own personal happiness before she'd do that to you.'

She was doing it now, he could have told her. Carrying on with this house, still keeping the home fires burning so the girls felt secure until they'd truly flown the nest.

And it was something he was going to have to take on board. Was he prepared to welcome the girls into his home, as well as Annie and his son?

Yes, he realised in surprise. Even after just one rather eventful evening, he found he was—because if he didn't, Annie would be unhappy, and he couldn't do that to her. Couldn't do it to any of them. God knows they were going to have enough to come to terms with without that.

He shot Vicky a crooked smile. 'I get the feeling we've been deliberately abandoned so we can have this chat,' he said softly, and she smiled back.

'We have. I asked them to. And I really am sorry—'

He grinned. 'Hey, Vicky, I'm cool with it, really. Don't worry.'

He patted her hand, stood up and stretched out the kinks in his neck and shoulders. 'I need to go home. Things to do. I'll see you round. You take care, now.'

'You, too. And, for the record, I'm really pleased for Annie. She looks kind of lit up inside, you know? And it's been so long since I've seen that, if I ever have. So thanks, if it's your doing. And good luck.'

His grin slipped a little. 'Thanks.'

He went out and closed the door softly, sucked in a breath and let it go, then turned to find Annie standing just feet away, her eyes filled with tears.

'Thank you,' she whispered almost silently. 'Thank you for being so kind to her.'

He ushered her into the kitchen, pushing the door closed behind them. The lights were out, and as she reached for them he stilled her hand, wrapped it in his and cradled it against his heart and with his other hand, he threaded his fingers through her hair, anchored her head and kissed her very, very thoroughly.

Then he lifted his head a fraction, propped his forehead on hers and sighed softly.

'I need to go,' he murmured.

'I know. I need to get to bed. I've got a lot to do tomorrow. Thank you for letting Stephen win—'

His finger found her lips, shushing her silently. 'Leave the kid his moment of glory,' he murmured. 'The next time he'll have to try a lot, lot harder. Right, I'm going. I'll see you on Monday—damn, no I won't. I'm in Norfolk. I'll see you on Tuesday. In fact, what are you doing on Tuesday evening?'

'Tuesday? That's chess club. Cooking, then, until eight.'

'Fancy playing hookey?'

'Hookey?'

He nodded. 'I'll cook for you. I'll pick you up at six. Be hungry.'

And, with a quick kiss to the tip of her nose, he let himself out of the back door and went home while he could still drag himself away.

*   *   *

Tuesday took for ever to come. Crazy how much she was looking forward to it. Grace and Jackie and Chris came in for lunch, Chris juggling the baby, and they took one look at her and sat her down and pumped her for information.

'So, how's it going?' Jackie asked. 'Has he asked you out?'

'Have you asked him out?' Chris said with a grin. 'I wouldn't leave a little thing like that to chance!'

She pulled a face. 'He's had supper at mine three times now—all with the chess in mind, of course—so yes, in a manner of speaking I have asked him out.'

'And?'

'And what?'

Grace rolled her eyes. 'And has he asked you?'

She felt herself colour slightly. 'Um—he's cooking for me tonight.'

'Where? In the flat upstairs? I hope the kitchen's perked up since the last time I saw it—it was in a skip!'

'Jackie, don't be silly.'

They were sitting looking at her expectantly, and she realised she didn't really know the answer.

'His house, I imagine.'

'Which is where?'

She shrugged. 'I have no idea,' she admitted. 'None at all. Can't be far.'

And she felt a sudden flutter of panic. She was going out for the evening with a man who was almost a stranger, to an unknown destination—good grief, there were names for people like her. Starting with naïve, and foolish, and ending with idiot.

And yet somehow she knew she was safe.

And anyway, he wasn't a stranger. Ruth had known him for years and said he was one of the kindest men she'd ever met, and the way he'd been with the kids on Saturday night backed that up.

But nevertheless, a little shiver of something—anticipation? Dread? Excitement?—ran over her skin.

'Are you going straight from here?'

She nodded, and Grace sat bolt upright. 'You can't! You need to go home and freshen up. Shower, change, shave your legs, put on your best underwear—'

'Grace!' she hissed, glancing over her shoulder and hoping all the rest of her customers were stone deaf, but Grace was unabashed.

'I'll babysit the tearoom for you. You go—what time do you want me back here? Four? That give you long enough?'

'Tons—'

'So use it wisely. Right, girls. What's she going to wear?'

'What are you going to eat now, more to the point—'

Jackie shot her an astonished look. 'What could possibly be more to the point than that? He's to die for, Annie. You need to dress up, woman. Glad rags. This needs planning like a military campaign.'

'He's probably planning beans on toast,' she protested weakly, but the girls were up and running, and before she knew what was what they'd got her house key off her and were gone, leaving her with the baby and the mess on the table while they plundered her wardrobe.

'Right,' Grace said when they came back a few minutes later. 'We've put a selection out on your bed. And you will be vetted when I've shut up shop. Here's your key. I need to shoot.'

'What about lunch?'

She flapped her hand at Annie. 'No time. Things to do before four. I'll see you then. Bye, girls.'

She zipped out, leaving Jackie and Chris plotting while the baby waved her arms around and smiled happily.

Oh, to be so young and free, Annie thought wistfully, and it wasn't just the baby she was thinking of...

'I can't wear them!'

She looked at the clothes the girls had left out for her and laughed a little frantically. A clingy dress, a pair of evening trousers and a slinky top, a clingy jumper—what was it with the clingy stuff?—a skirt she'd been meaning to throw out for ages because it was too short, a pair of outrageous little shoes with wickedly high heels that she could hardly stand in, never mind walk—she couldn't wear any of this lot!

She put on the trousers and the jumper, but it just looked like something she'd wear every day. A bit dressier, but nothing special. And suddenly, for no very sensible reason and a lot of rather silly ones, she wanted to look special.

For him.

She pulled off the jumper and trousers, slipped the dress over her head and shimmied it down her hips. She'd never worn it. She'd bought it ages ago for a Christmas do, but then they hadn't gone. It must be nearly two years old. She wriggled her feet into the shoes, turned to the mirror—

And froze.

Was that her? That woman with the sparkle in her eyes and the glow in her cheeks and the soft, full lips that were rosy with anticipation?

The doorbell rang, and she stared at herself in horror. No! He couldn't be here this early! But he was. She looked down and there he was, in the front garden, chatting to Grace, the scheming little she-rat.

Oh, well, there was no time to do anything about it now. She sucked in her stomach, straightened her shoulders and checked herself in front of the mirror, then slapped on the merest touch of lip gloss to complete her make-up and picked her way carefully through the abandoned clothes and down the stairs.

'Coming!' she called and, grabbing her coat, she dived into it and buttoned it before opening the door, bag slung casually over her shoulder.

Grace narrowed her eyes and tilted her head slightly, but then her eyes slid down, clocked the shoes and she smirked. Annie reached out and took the key and thanked Grace, then turned to Michael.

'Ready when you are,' she said, closing the door firmly behind her, and Grace winked and mouthed 'Good luck!', wiggled her fingers and ran across to the car park in the middle of the square.

'Where's your car?'

'Next to Grace's,' he said, and she looked.

OK. Neither of them was the respectable and middle-of-the-road Volvo estate he'd been using all last week. On one side was a grubby but newish off-roader, the other side was a—oh, boy. Something much classier. Gorgeous, in a sleek and sinuous and utterly outrageous way. But which—?

'The DB9,' he said. 'It's my baby—a lunatic bit of self-indulgence. I thought you might like it.' He pressed a plip on the remote and the Aston Martin's indicators flashed. Well, she conceded, if he'd bothered to break out the flash car, maybe Grace had been right about the clothes. And he'd probably had the meal catered. He was always saying how he never got round to cooking. Suddenly she didn't feel quite so overdressed.

He opened the car door, seated her, pulled down the belt and leant over her to clip it, his face just inches from hers, his hand warm against her hip.

'OK?' he murmured, and she nodded.

She didn't dare trust herself to speak.

He closed the door with one of those clunks that whispered quality, and went round to the driver's side, sliding in beside her and clipping on his seat belt before firing up the engine.

A fabulous, deliciously throaty burble echoed through the bodywork and made her shiver. As he eased out of the car park, through the village and on to the open road, he opened it up and the burble turned to a sexy, full-blooded growl that took her breath away.

He didn't exceed the speed limit, nor did he take her out of her comfort-zone, but the coiled power of the car was there, and somehow that was enough.

Then he eased back on the throttle, turned down a track and guided the car slowly alongside the hedge until they rounded a bend and there it was.

'It's a barn!' she said, her eyes wide. 'Oh, Michael! I didn't know you lived in a barn! Oh, I'm so envious!'

'Your house is gorgeous,' he said, but there was a question in his voice and she answered it.

'It's not my house. It's Liz and Roger's house, their dream, their home, their sanctuary. It's not mine. I feel as if I'm living in a museum sometimes. Someone else's image of the perfect house. But this—'

He opened the door and ushered her in, reached out to touch the switch that brought the lights up slowly, illuminating every nook and cranny of the interior.

It seemed to go up for miles. She shook her head wordlessly, taking it all in. The heavy, twisted oak beams, the steel walkway that crossed the central space and linked the two ends upstairs, the open-plan living area that flowed naturally from the sitting end through to the kitchen—and in the central section a wall of glass on each side that soared all the way up to the eaves of the roof.

Through the one they were facing she could see lights twinkling in the gathering gloom. 'Is that the church spire in the village?' she said, and he nodded.

'Yes.'

'That's just on the other side of the market square to the house, behind the shops.'

'I know.'

'How amazing. What a fabulous view you must have in daylight.'

'It is. It's gorgeous.' His hands cupped her arms gently. 'Here, let me take your coat,' he murmured, and she let it slip from her shoulders into his waiting hands, holding her breath for his reaction to the dress.

She wasn't disappointed. He inhaled sharply and, as she turned, his eyes flared and then were swiftly controlled.

'You look beautiful,' he said huskily, his voice sounding more gravelly even than usual. 'Come on through. You can sit here and talk to me while I cook. We're having beef Stroganoff.'

They were, as well. Properly cooked, with meltingly tender fillet steak and soured cream and onions sweated in butter, served with wild rice and baby-leaf salad.

She perched on a stool at the granite-topped island, propped her chin on her hands and watched him work.

'Here,' he said, pouring a slug of red wine for her and sliding it towards her. 'Taste that.'

'I'm not much of a wine buff.'

'You'll like this one. My godfather gave it to me yesterday. One of his friends owns a very old vineyard that's been in the family for generations, and he sent him a case.'

It was gorgeous. Unbelievable. It slid down her throat like velvet, leaving a wild burst of flavours that brought her eyes wide open then let them drift shut on the experience.

'Mmm,' she said, and he grinned.

'Said you'd like it. It's not commercially available. Friends and family only, and they're pretty good friends, so every now and then he gets a treat.'

'And you're wasting it on me when you're driving me?'

He shook his head. 'I'm not bothered. I don't drink a lot. I can have a glass with you, and if there's any left I can finish it later.'

'If there's any left?' she said with a chuckle. 'I'm hardly going to drink the other however-many glasses, even if it is sublime! I might have two, at a push.'

'Then I'll certainly get to enjoy it later. That's fine. It's quality, not quantity.'

He stirred the onions in the pan, came back to the island and smiled at her. 'OK?'

'Wonderful. But I feel curiously redundant. Can I do anything?'

He shook his head. 'Just talk to me.'

So she did, in between watching the quick, precise movements of his hands as he tore and sliced and whisked. And she found herself wondering what those hands would feel like on her body, just as he dipped his finger in the salad dressing and sucked it, then dipped it back in and held it out to her to taste.

Their eyes locked, and he leant over, holding his finger to her lips in silent invitation.

How could she refuse?

She opened her mouth, closed it round his fingertip and suckled gently. Heat exploded through her, and as she looked up at him she saw that same heat reflected in his eyes.

She straightened up, dragged in a breath, looked away.

'Um—it's fine,' she said.

'Estate-bottled olive oil from the same vineyard, and they

also make the balsamic vinegar,' he said, his voice so husky she could hardly hear the words.

Or was that because of the roaring in her ears?

She turned away, clutching the fabulously rare and delicious wine in front of her with both hands, like a cross to ward off evil spirits.

What was it she'd told Ruth about not wanting a man in her life? And yet here she was, just two weeks later, burning for him so fiercely she thought she'd die in the fire.

His hands closed over her shoulders, turning her gently towards him. The wine vanished, and then she was in his arms.

'Relax. I'm only going to hold you,' he murmured, his voice low and soothing, and she let herself lean into him, resting her head against his chest and listening to the deep, even rhythm of his heartbeat.

And gradually her body relaxed, the tension easing, shifting as she accepted this thing that was happening to her—to them—and let herself acclimatise.

'OK now?'

She nodded. 'I'm sorry. I'm not used to this. It's been a while since I've dated anyone.'

His laugh was gruff and warm, and he hugged her. 'That makes two of us,' he said, and let her go, returning to the onions and mushrooms, testing them, then throwing the rice into a pan of boiling water.

'Can I lay the table?' she asked.

'Done,' he said, and she turned and stared.

How could she have missed it? A long, plain wooden table and tall, graceful chairs, set in the centre of the vaulted section, was laid with sleek stainless steel cutlery and slate place mats arranged at right angles to each other at one end, slender white candles waiting for a flame to work their magic.

So simple. So clean, so pure, so unfussy.

So Michael.

And a rose. Just one, in a tall, slim glass, beside one of the places. A white rose, touched with cream, the bud about to burst.

Tears filled her eyes. 'You're really spoiling me, aren't you?' she said, suddenly fiercely glad that she'd worn the dress and not caring if this thing was going too fast for common sense. Since when had that had anything to do with anything?

'I'd like to,' he said, and there was something utterly sincere in his voice, utterly trustworthy and decent and honourable. It made her feel safe—oddly, since she was poised on the brink of a precipice, staring out over the unknown.

He picked up a remote control, and soft music flowed through the room, romantic vocals designed to set the mood. The lights dimmed, he picked up the dishes and put them on the table, then held out his hand to her, his mouth kicking up in that one-sided, curiously sexy smile.

'Dinner is served, *madame*.'

A shiver ran over her. Etienne had called her *mademoiselle*, in just the same way. She was falling for Michael as she'd fallen for him, headlong without thought or caution.

Was that how she was destined to fall in love every time?

She held out her hand to him, letting him take it and settle her in the chair. He lit the candles, lifted the lid on the dishes and she caught the scent of the steaming, fragrant rice and the rich, creamy Stroganoff.

It tasted wonderful. The flavours, the textures, meltingly tender and rich and smooth, the salad a sweet, fresh counterpoint.

She shook her head, smiled wordlessly at him and cleared her plate.

'More?'

'Absolutely. I'll probably put on a half a stone, but who cares?'

He chuckled. 'I'll take that as a compliment,' he said, and piled another helping on each of their plates.

'If you can cook like that, why on earth do you need to eat in my scruffy little tearoom?' she asked in amazement as she set her fork down for the second time.

'Because the food is wonderful.'

'No. *That* was wonderful. My food is wholesome.'

'Exactly. That's what you need on a daily basis. If I ate like that all the time, I'd probably have a heart attack before I'm forty.'

The words stopped her in her tracks, and she looked away, sucking in a suddenly much-needed breath. 'I don't think that's always why people have heart attacks,' she said quietly, and he groaned and put down his glass.

'Oh, Annie, I'm so sorry. I can't believe I said that.'

She looked back at him, smiling to reassure him. 'Don't be silly. I was just feeling guilty because the whole time I've been with you I've hardly given Roger a thought.'

Well, it was plausible, at least. In fact she'd suddenly considered the possibility of losing him and been shocked at the stab of grief that had pierced her heart. It was nothing to do with Roger and everything to do with this man and what he was coming to mean to her.

And suddenly she couldn't lie to him.

'That's not true,' she said, before she could bottle out. 'Actually, it was the thought of you dying—of anything— that shook me. Apparently you're coming to mean something to me—something I hadn't expected. I know you were joking, but—it's just—I've lost two men already. I know it happens. I'm sorry, I'm being silly, spoiling things—'

'Annie, I'm not going to die,' he said, leaning towards

her and taking her suddenly cold hand in his. 'I promise you, I have no intention of dying—at least not for a damn long while.'

'What about your headaches?' she said, and his mouth twisted into a wry smile.

'They're just the aftermath of my accident,' he told her. 'I had neck injuries as well as facial injuries. Sometimes, if I do something stupid or get stressed out, I get a migraine. The osteopath fixes it, it's not a problem.'

She nodded, reassured about something she hadn't real- ised was troubling her. 'Liz had headaches,' she said, and he sighed.

'Of course. I'm sorry, I didn't think about that, either.'

'Why should you? It's over—past. Let's talk about some- thing else.'

'Such as?'

'You,' she said promptly. 'So how long have you got before this heart attack you aren't planning to have at forty?' she asked, swirling the wine in her glass as she studied him shamelessly.

He chuckled and eased back in his chair. 'Two years. I'm thirty-eight.'

Strange. He looked older, and yet not. Maybe it was just because of all that had happened to him, but the touch of silver at his temples and the lived-in face were older than the body.

Vicky was right. He was male. Macho. Dangerous.

But only to her heart.

Their eyes locked and, despite all the things she wanted to know about him, she couldn't string a single coherent thought together. All she could do was feel—

He pushed back his chair and stood up, holding out a hand to her.

'Dance with me,' he murmured, and without argument or question she stood and went into his arms.

Common sense reared its head briefly. 'This is crazy,' she whispered. 'I have to get back for Stephen.'

'You're quite safe. It's quarter past seven. I'll have to take you back at a quarter to eight. When I make love to you, Annie, I'm going to want more than half an hour to do it.'

When I make love to you.

Not if.

When.

Oh, yes. Please. It's been so long.

Her body seemed to fit so perfectly against his. Their legs meshed seamlessly, thigh to thigh, hip to hip, their bodies swaying together in perfect harmony.

She felt his lips trace a slow, leisurely trail down from her brow, over her cheekbone, across her ear and down to the sensitive skin of her throat. She lifted her head, allowing him access to the hollow where his touch was making the pulse leap.

His tongue stroked it, dragging a groan from her aching, longing body, and with a murmured, 'Shh,' he rocked her gently against him, bringing their hips closer together so she could feel exactly what this was doing to him, too.

A whimper escaped from her mouth, and he lifted his head and stared down into her eyes, then slowly, achingly slowly, he lowered his mouth to hers.

That was when she realised she'd never been kissed in her life before. Not by Etienne, not by Roger, certainly, and not even by Michael in that slow, thorough exploration on Saturday night.

Because this kiss was a promise, a vow, a total surrender of his heart to hers.

And hers to his.

Finally he lifted his head, his eyes dark with need and laced with regret. 'I have to take you home,' he said hoarsely.

'No,' she moaned. 'Please, no.'

'I have to,' he said. 'Stephen—'

And that was enough.

There would be time for them. But she couldn't let her son down, and she was shocked at how close she'd come to it.

She took a step back out of his arms, and then another.

'Of course,' she agreed. 'We'll go now.'

While we still can...

CHAPTER SEVEN

WOW.

He'd been *that* close.

He dropped into the sofa, a glass of Antoine's excellent Pinot Noir in his hand, and closed his eyes.

She'd tasted of wine and cream, and honey from the salad dressing, and her body had felt so good—so soft, slender and yet lush, full in all the right places.

She'd changed, filled out. From breast-feeding?

The thought dragged a groan from the bottom of his lungs. He wanted her. Needed her.

He squeezed his eyes tight against the sudden prickle of tears. He'd waited so long, loved her for ever. And it seemed she loved him, too.

She hadn't said so, but he'd felt it. That kiss had said it all, and it was more than chemistry. It was recognition, he was sure of it. Their souls had been reunited in that kiss, and finally, after the agony of the past nine years, he allowed himself to dare to hope.

And it was time to tell her the truth, and hope she'd forgive him for all the lies and deception of the past and present.

'I love you, Annie,' he said softly. 'Whatever happens, I love you. I always have, and I always will.'

He opened his eyes again, staring out over the valley to the lights of the village in the distance. He could see the floodlights illuminating the church, and just down and to the left was her house. He couldn't tell which room she

118

was in, but if he got out the binoculars he could work it out, even in the dark.

He didn't, though. He just waited, and eventually the lights went out.

'Sleep tight, my darling,' he murmured.

Then, draining his glass, he went up to bed.

'Hi, Sport.'

'Hi. I'm starving. Can we play chess?'

'Maybe later. Haven't you got homework to do?' Annie asked, coming over to the round table by the window where Michael had been for the past half hour and where Stephen was now busy making himself at home after school.

'Not tonight. Mr Greaves was sick, and we had a supply teacher. She let us off. She's cool, I like her.'

'I'll bet,' Annie muttered. 'So did you go swimming this afternoon then?'

He shook his head and pulled a face. 'No. We couldn't. She's not a lifesaver. I told her we didn't need a lifesaver— well, I don't, anyway, but she wouldn't change her mind.'

He looked so glum and crestfallen. Michael had vowed he was going to have less to do with him until he'd talked to Annie, but there was a pool at his house, just sitting there waiting—

'Are you a good swimmer?' he asked, and Stephen nodded.

'He swims like a fish,' Annie said. 'And he needs to burn off energy, so I hope you did something energetic instead?' she added, turning her attention to her son.

'We had to be trees,' he said, disgust in his voice. Michael nearly laughed aloud, and there was a twinkle in Annie's eyes, quickly disguised. He looked away as she spoke, biting the inside of his cheek to trap the laugh.

'I thought she was cool?' she was saying.

'Only because of the homework.'

Michael glanced up and met her eyes again, then glanced at Stephen and jerked his head slightly.

To his relief she understood. 'Stephen, why don't you go and wash your hands before you have something to eat?' she suggested, and with a sigh he slid off his chair and headed for the cloakroom.

Annie cocked her head on one side. 'Why did you want him out of the way?'

He smiled wryly. 'I've got a pool at the barn,' he told her. 'It's heated, it's safe and, unlike the partly cool teacher, I *am* a lifesaver. I could take him over now, let him swim and give him a game of chess, then you could come over when you finish here and we could have supper. Well, if you bring something to eat we could. I've got salad but not much else. And I might be able to find another glass of that wine for you.'

Stephen was coming back, and she hesitated, doubt in her eyes. 'You will take care of him?'

'With my life,' he vowed. 'Nothing will happen to him while I'm looking after him, I promise.'

Still she wavered, and he sensed the struggle in her, and the moment that he won.

She nodded. 'OK. Stephen, do you want to go swimming with Michael at his house?'

The boy's eyes widened with delight. 'You've got a pool? Wicked!'

'So is that a yes?'

'I think so,' Annie said drily. 'You'll need to go home and get your swimming things. Michael, could you go with him? Do you mind?'

'Of course not. And when you come over, you could bring yours and join us in the pool.'

She looked flustered for a second. 'I have to cook some time this week. I'll be running out.'

'I'll help you later.'

'My silent partner?'

He laughed softly. 'I can't promise to be silent, but at least you know I can cook.'

Amongst other things.

Heat flared in her eyes and she looked hastily away. 'I'll see you guys later, then. About six or so.'

'Can you remember the way?'

She nodded. 'Of course.'

He ruffled his son's hair and stood up. 'Come on then, Tiger. Let's go.'

Annie watched them through the window, her son and the man who was coming to mean so much to her.

He was wonderful with the boy—just what Stephen needed.

Just what she needed—

'No!'

He stopped Stephen on the kerb with a firm hand on his collar, just before he ran out in front of a car. Her heart in her mouth, she was on the point of rushing out to tell him off when Michael shook his head and said something. Stephen hung his head, then muttered what looked like a slightly shamefaced apology; then Michael reached out and took his shoulder—not his hand, because he wouldn't have allowed that liberty—and steered him across the road and in through her gate without any further incident.

'So where are they going?'

'Michael's taking him swimming. He's got a pool at his house.' She turned towards Grace and found the woman eyeing her with unashamed curiosity.

'Indeed?' she said slowly. 'Wicked.'

'That's what Stephen said. Are you on your own?'

'No, Jack's just parking and Chris is joining us.' Grace grinned. 'So how was dinner? I liked the car.'

'What was it?' Chris asked, appearing at her elbow.

'An Aston Martin DB9.'

Chris whistled softly. 'Wow, the guy has class. Can he cook?'

She nodded slowly, remembering the food, the wine, the candlelight and soft music. Dancing with him.

The kiss.

'Yes, he can cook.' She was pretty damn certain he could do everything.

Especially that—

Colouring, she turned back to the kitchen. 'Tea?'

'Mmm. And the rest,' Grace said. 'You don't get away with that.'

Annie sighed. She didn't imagine for a moment that she would!

'So,' Jackie said the moment she sat down with them, 'tell us all. What did he cook you?'

'Don't be boring. What's the house like?' Chris asked, and Grace rolled her eyes.

'You lot! Talk about the trivia,' she said, then lowered her voice to a conspiratorial whisper. 'Can he kiss?'

Annie sighed. 'Beef Stroganoff the proper way with meltingly tender rare fillet steak, served on a bed of wild rice with a side salad, the most gorgeous estate-bottled Pinot Noir from a friend of his godfather that was quite amazing, a lovely, lovely converted barn with stunning views over the valley towards the village, and yes. Absolutely.'

Grace sighed with contentment.

'Thought so.'

'What?' Jackie said, clearly lost.

'He can kiss. I knew it.'

All six eyes swivelled back to Annie, and she felt her colour mount.

'That was all! It was just a little kiss.'

Like the north pole in January was just a little chilly.

Chris looked out to the car park and watched as Michael backed the Volvo out of a space and drove slowly away, Stephen strapped into the rear passenger seat.

'Interesting.'

'What?' Annie asked, craning her neck and starting to worry.

'He's put him in the back,' Chris explained. 'If you put them in the front without a booster seat the seat belt's too high on their necks until they're about twelve. Not something you'd expect a bachelor to think of.'

'I'm amazed you let him go with Michael.' That from Grace, who'd obviously moved on from the kiss, to Annie's relief.

'I haven't had a choice about letting him do things with other people. I'm in here so much that I either have him here bored to death with me or I let him get on with his life with someone else.'

And worry myself sick the entire time, she added silently.

'He'll be fine,' Chris said gently. 'Michael's thoughtful and intelligent and considerate.'

'And he can kiss, and he's got a great sense of humour, he doesn't smoke and he's got a lovely, lovely barn. So when's the big day?'

Annie laughed and swatted Jackie gently. 'Give me time to breathe! I've only known him just over a week!'

'Nine days, seven hours and fifteen minutes,' Grace said smugly.

Annie already knew that. It said something about what a sad, desperate widow she was turning into.

'If you say so,' she said, and dragged the conversation into safer waters. 'What can I take over there for supper?'

Their eyes locked on hers again. 'You're going for supper?'

'Again?'

'Two nights running?'

So much for safe!

'That was cool!'

Michael grinned and threw the boy a towel. 'Here—you can go and shower and get dressed. We can have a game of chess before your mum gets here, and maybe we can swim again later if she wants to.'

'Excellent!'

He showed him how the shower worked in the wet room off the lobby by the pool, then left him to it. He hovered in earshot, though, preparing the salad in the kitchen, and when he heard the water stop he went up to his room and showered and dressed in record time. He'd promised Annie no harm would come to her son, and although he knew he was taking it to ridiculous extremes, as far as he was concerned that included slipping in the shower.

He'd also promised Annie a swim, but after the exhausting chase up and down the pool and rough and tumble he'd had with Stephen, he was more than ready to slump into a chair with a glass of Antoine's wine and put his feet up.

All that exercise on top of damn all sleep was a killer. Chess was just about all he felt he could manage.

'OK, Sport?'

Stephen nodded. He was standing in the dining room, his hair spiking wildly, peering out over the valley. 'Is that our village?' he asked, pointing, and Michael nodded.

'Yup. See the church spire? Your house must be down and to the left a bit.'

'I can't see it.'

'That might be because the lights aren't on, if your mum isn't at home yet,' he replied, resisting the urge to ruffle the boy's hair for the sake of it. 'You can see it better in the daytime.'

'Can I come and swim again? At the weekend?' And then his face lit up. 'Oh. Can't come at the weekend. I'm going to Bristol with Edward for Tom's birthday! Ed's dad's driving us down on Saturday morning early, because he's got a meeting or something, and we're going to an assault course on Saturday and then we're going to have pizza and go to the cinema, and Mum's bringing us back on Sunday. It's going to be so wicked.'

'In Bristol?' he said.

Stephen nodded. 'Tom lives there now. He moved just after my birthday. I haven't seen him for ages.'

Since July or thereabouts, Michael calculated. Ages? He didn't know what ages was. Ages was Stephen's lifetime. All of it, from the moment of conception—

'Fancy a game of chess?'

'Yeah! Wonder if I'll beat you again?'

'Not if I have anything to say about it!' Michael said drily. 'Being beaten once by an eight-year-old is hard. Being beaten more than that is downright careless.'

'Maybe I'm just dead good?'

Michael snorted. 'Maybe you just got lucky.'

'We'll see, shall we?' Stephen said with a cheeky grin, and Michael allowed himself one masculine and sporting ruffle of the dark, damp hair so like his own.

'Oh, I think I'm ready for you.'

'You reckon?'

'I reckon. Bring it on, Tiger. Let's see what you're made of.'

He was improving, there was no question about it, but he wasn't there yet. He wouldn't catch Michael without co-operation for a while, but then he had a heck of a lot of catching up to do.

Months. Months and months of sitting over a chessboard or a computer waiting for his face to heal, for his ribs to recover and the plaster casts to come off his arms, for his voice to come back to something approaching normal after his throat had been kicked in.

Months when there'd been nothing else to do but lie and watch television or think about David and what had gone wrong.

Months haunted by David's death, by Ruth's long, slow road to recovery, by the memory of Annie's tears when he'd told her he loved her just before he'd left her for the last time.

Months he didn't want to remember or go through ever again—

'Check.'

He sucked in a sharp breath, stared down at the board and frowned. Hell's teeth. He was losing it. Getting sloppy.

He studied the pieces for a moment, eyes narrowed, and then made his move. Stephen would have no choice but to do *that*, and then he could do *that*, and that would be it. He'd have him.

Ego saved for another day.

'Your move.'

The outside lights came on, and he pushed back the chair and went to the door, opening it and standing there, propped against the doorframe, watching her approach.

'Is he OK?'

He smiled. 'Of course he's OK. We've had a great time. I'm just thrashing him at chess. Everything all right with you?'

She smiled up at him, her face softening. 'It is now.'

His heart seemed to swell in his chest, and drawing the door to behind him, he lowered his head and stole a light, lingering kiss.

He felt the door open behind him and lifted his head, just as Stephen came out.

'Have you brought supper? I'm *starving*!'

'Mum, you have to see the pool! It's brilliant!'

He grabbed her hand and towed her through the house, past the dining room where they'd eaten that amazingly romantic meal and where he'd danced with her and kissed her oh, so beautifully, through the kitchen and off through a doorway at the end into a lobby. Then on, through the lobby, and into a huge room, another barn in its own right. And there, filling the centre, was a clear, still pool that gleamed in the light streaming through the windows from the floodlights in the courtyard outside.

Michael reached round beside her and touched a switch, and light flooded the room—under the water, up into the beams, through the plants—everywhere, but so subtle, so carefully planned that the sources were all but invisible.

'I didn't cover it—I wasn't sure if you'd want to go in later.'

She did. She wanted to so much it was almost an ache, but she had so much to do, and swimming practically naked with Michael in this somehow very intimate setting was not one of the things on her to-do list. Her wish-list, however, was a different matter!

'That's my favourite bit,' he said, pointing to a recess, and she saw a huge round whirlpool. 'My treat, after a long workout, as a reward for being good. And it's brilliant for getting the kinks out when I've been writing hard.'

It looked wonderfully, enormously inviting, and she felt herself wavering.

She dragged her eyes away and smiled down at Stephen. 'I bet you had loads of fun.'

'I did—and Michael says I can come again, but not the weekend because I'm at Tom's, so it'll have to be another time—'

'Hey, hey, slow down! Maybe Michael doesn't want you constantly underfoot. In fact, let's eat and get you home. You're getting over-excited and you've got school tomorrow.'

'He's fine. He's a kid. He's allowed to be enthusiastic. So—does it appeal? Do I leave the cover off?'

She hesitated, and he grinned and dropped an arm round her shoulders, hugging her briefly before releasing her and turning away.

'I'll leave it—keep your options open. Did you manage to find anything for us to eat?'

She nodded, following him reluctantly away from the inviting water and back into the kitchen. 'I brought some soup and quiche and a few slices of cheesecake. Is that OK? Not quite up to your standard, I'm afraid, but it was the best I could do—'

'It sounds great. I don't suppose you brought corn bread?'

She would have teased him, but he saw the indulgent smile just as she felt it reach her eyes. 'Now, what do you think?'

If Stephen hadn't been there, she thought he would have hugged her again. Instead he winked, and she felt the impact of it right down to her toes.

'Plates?' she said, getting practical, and he put the crockery out on the central island, retrieved the salad from his huge American fridge-freezer and put it on the table.

'Any of that dressing left?' she asked, and he nodded.

'In the fridge.'

She opened it, and laughed. It was vast—and almost empty. Some cheese, a tired wedge of melon, a few wrinkled grapes and a plastic milk carton—semi-skimmed, she noticed—were about all that was in it, except a few vegetables lurking in the drawers at the bottom and the remains of last night's rice under cling wrap.

'Good job you've got such a big fridge,' she teased, and he grinned.

'I bought it for the water chiller. I love iced water. Drink gallons of it.'

'Can we have one, Mum?' Stephen asked. 'Look, it's cool. You get a glass and push it here, and you get cold water, and if you push it here you get ice!'

She turned to Michael and gave a wry smile. 'You seem to be a big hit with my son. Everything you have is either cool or brilliant.'

His smile was a little wary—or was that just because his mouth didn't move quite right? She wasn't sure, but it didn't seem to reach his eyes.

'We aim to please,' he said lightly, and turned away, but not before she saw a slight grimace cross his face.

'Are you OK?'

He nodded. 'Just ache a bit. We swam for a long time. I might have twinged something.'

She had the distinct feeling he was lying, but she didn't push it, and by the time the soup was heated and the meal was on the table, his smile was firmly back in place and Stephen was chattering nineteen to the dozen to cover any potential silences.

She told herself she was imagining it, but when Stephen

wanted to swim again right after supper, he shook his head. 'Only if your mother wants to. It's getting late, and she's got things to do.'

Outstaying their welcome? Suddenly it seemed like it.

She met his eyes. 'I'm sorry. We've taken you over—'

'No. Annie, I didn't mean that,' he said, apparently reading her mind. 'I just don't want you ending up exhausted because you've had to burn the candle at both ends. You're more than welcome, both of you.' He glanced away from her to Stephen.

'We've got a game of chess to finish. Why don't you go and make your move?'

'I did. It's your turn.'

'Right. I'll do that, then while I clear up you can make your next move, and if your mother wants to swim, she can be changing while we finish the game. If not, well, whatever. We can have a cup of coffee and you can go.'

His eyes were back on her again, putting the ball back in her court. Then he went over to the sitting area, stared down at the chessboard on the table in the middle, moved a piece and came back to her, leaving Stephen there to contemplate his next attempted coup.

'I'd like you to stay a while,' he murmured. 'You aren't overstaying your welcome, and I'm not trying to buy my way into your heart by spoiling your son.'

She frowned. 'I didn't think you were. The thought hadn't even occurred to me. I was just concerned that you must be getting sick of him.'

A strange emotion flickered in his eyes and was gone. 'Not at all. Did you bring your things?'

She nodded.

'So, do you want to swim?'

'Is the hot tub warm?'

His smile was slow and gentle. 'No. It's hot. It's gorgeous, and it'll do you good. Go and change and slide into it and wallow. I'll come and join you when I've thrashed the pipsqeak. The changing room's just off the lobby on the right.'

She nodded, picked up her bag and went through to the changing room.

Tumbled stone tiles covered the walls, the floor was warm slate, and there was a wet room that looked as if it had a drenching shower. No expense spared, then, she thought, and suddenly realised just how rich he must be.

How totally out of her league.

What on *earth* was she doing here with him? Why was he interested in her? Of all the women he could have, why her, for heaven's sake? He was gorgeous! A real catch.

Why her?

She changed into her discreet and all-covering black chain-store costume, wrapped her towel around her like a sarong and headed out to the pool room.

He'd turned the lights on for her, and the whirlpool was bubbling gently. She dipped her toe in, sighed and followed it, sinking under the foaming water with a blissful sigh. Stretching her arms out along the rim, she laid back, shut her eyes and let go.

He stood there for a moment watching her. Stephen hadn't wanted to swim again—not once he'd discovered there was satellite TV. He was settled on the sofa in front of a cartoon channel, and Michael didn't think it would be long before his eyes drooped.

He wasn't alone.

He'd brought coffee on a tray, and he set it down at the edge of the tub and slid into the water beside her.

'Hi, gorgeous,' he murmured and, leaning over, he dropped a kiss on her lips.

Her eyes fluttered open and she smiled at him sleepily.

'I'm sorry—I must have dozed off.'

'You're tired. That's fine. I've brought you coffee.'

He handed her a cup, and she sat up straighter and took it from him. He shifted so he was opposite her, watching her over the top of his cup. Their legs brushed, and her eyes flew up to meet his, automatically pulling her legs away a fraction.

He went after them, hooking his heels behind hers and pulling them back towards him, then threading his legs around hers so they were enclosed, all the time holding her eyes with his.

Heat flared in them, and she swallowed slightly.

He put his cup down, reached under the water and pulled her feet on to his lap, then one at a time he massaged her feet and ankles, easing out the strain of standing all day.

'Oh, that's bliss,' she groaned, putting her own cup down and sliding further under the water, her hands locked on the rim to stop her sliding right under. He changed feet, and her toes brushed against his groin, making him suck in his breath sharply. The urge to pull her across the water and into his arms nearly overwhelmed him, but he concentrated on the other foot, reminding himself that her son...*their* son—was just a few metres away and didn't need that liberal an education.

He just hoped he didn't have to get out of the water in front of her any time soon.

'So who won the chess?' she asked lazily, and he gave a strained chuckle.

'Who do you think? I'm not letting him get away with that twice.'

'What's he doing?'

'Watching cartoons on the telly. I think he's nearly asleep.'

'Good. That means I don't need to feel guilty for keeping him up.'

'You could stay here,' he suggested out of the blue. 'I've got plenty of bedrooms.'

Including mine, with a very large, very empty bed just crying out for you—

'No.' She shook her head. 'That's too much. Anyway, the cat will sulk.'

'The cat always sulks. I've never seen that cat when it's not sulking,' he said with a grin.

'Horrible cat. It acquired us five years ago. I suppose at some point I'm going to stop thinking of it as a stray.'

He laughed and rubbed his thumbs lightly over the soles of her feet, his fingers curled loosely over the top of her toes. 'OK now?'

She nodded. 'Lovely. Thank you. They really ache some days with all the standing.'

'I can imagine.' He tipped his head on one side. 'About the weekend.'

She shook her head. 'Stephen's in Bristol with a friend for an old schoolmate's birthday party. I have to drive down on Sunday and pick them up, and I'm open on Saturday. I won't have a weekend, I'm afraid.'

'I was thinking about Saturday night.'

She shook her head again. 'No. I can't do anything. I've got to make an early start on Sunday if I'm going to Bristol and back.'

'That's what I was going to say. If you could get someone to cover you for Saturday afternoon, we could go down and spend the night near there and bring the kids back on Sunday. There's a hotel just outside Cardiff with the most spectacular view across the city and over the bay, and the food's wonderful. This time of year I shouldn't think they'll be too busy, so they should have a couple of rooms.'

'A couple?'

Her eyes were worried.

'A couple. No strings, Annie. I'm not trying to sneak you away for a dirty weekend. I just thought you might like to share the driving, and get away for a night. We could go in the Volvo. It's a piece of cake to drive.'

'I know. Roger used to have one; it was lovely.' She nibbled her lip.

'Penny for them.'

She met his eyes squarely, then came out with something totally unexpected.

'Why me?' she said.

His heart lurched. Oh, this one was dead easy. Too easy, but he wasn't lying to her again. Never, if he had his way. This time, though, he didn't have to. He simply told her the truth.

'Because ever since I met you, I haven't been able to get you out of my head. You make my sun come out, my days worth living. I want you, Annie. I want a relationship with you—a full-on, proper, serious relationship. I want us to have time to get to know each other, to be sure it's what we both want, but as far as I'm concerned, it's the real thing and nothing's going to change that. I love you.'

She swallowed hard, looked away, looked back again, her eyes shimmering.

'That's the nicest thing anyone's ever said to me—but you still haven't answered my question.'

He shrugged. 'I can't. I don't know why you, in particular, but it is you, very definitely. I've never felt like this about another woman in my life. And I've never told another woman that I love her.'

She closed her eyes, and the threatening tears spilled over and slid down her cheeks.

'It's so quick,' she whispered.

He could have laughed out loud. Quick? They'd had nine years—but they hadn't really, and she was right. It was quick. It had been quick then, and it was no different now.

No different at all in one respect. She still didn't know who he really was—and that was something he was going to have to deal with very, very soon...

CHAPTER EIGHT

THEY went cross-country, avoiding the M25 and the M4 as long as possible. Their journey took them through the picturesque Cotswolds to Cheltenham, then through the Forest of Dean via Ross-on-Wye and down to Monmouth, picking up the M4 at Newport for the last stretch to Cardiff.

It was a beautiful day, and Annie found herself dozing, cosseted in the big comfortable passenger seat while Michael drove.

All the way.

He turned off the motorway just before six, cut through a few back roads and headed north again, then turned into the drive of the hotel and pulled up facing south with the hotel behind them.

And in front of them was the most fantastic view over Cardiff to the Bay, across the Bristol Channel and all the way to Weston-Super-Mare in the distance.

Lights were starting to come on, the sun low in the sky now, and an amazing sunset was streaking the clouds a stunning pink. Michael got out of the car, bent over and smiled at her.

'Come on. We can see the sunset from our rooms.'

'How do you know that?'

'Because I know which rooms we've been given.'

She opened the door and got out. 'How do you know? Have you stayed here before?'

He nodded. 'Several times. Ruth and I used it when we were researching in the area. I've set a book in this part of Wales.'

She remembered it. Remembered the vividly drawn characters, the banked emotions held back of necessity, the wild explosion of heat when those emotions were finally released. Was that what it would be like with him—?

'Come on.'

She went, following him as he picked up their cases as if they weighed nothing and headed for the steps.

'Mr Harding, welcome back. Here you are—your keys. Could you just sign there for me? Thank you. I hope you enjoy your stay. If there's anything you need, just give us a call.'

The receptionist slid the card keys across the desk to him, and he handed them to Annie and led the way through doors and down stairs and round the corner until she wondered why he'd be taking her on a tour of the basement; then at the end of the wide corridor he stopped.

'We've got these two in the corner,' he said, and taking the keys from her he opened one of the doors, ushering her in.

She didn't know what to expect, but it was amazing. Nothing like a basement, but at ground level, taking advantage, obviously, of the sloping site, and the room was stunning. Gorgeous. An enormous room, with a bathroom on one side as she entered it, hanging space and shelving on the other. As the room widened out, a huge double bed sat on one wall, with a sofa and chair beyond it arranged around French doors which led out on to a terrace.

Beyond the terrace the ground fell away again, and there stretched out in front of her was the most spectacular sky she'd ever seen.

'It's beautiful,' she said, unable to take her eyes off it, and he ushered her out of the doors and stood close behind her, his arm over her shoulder, pointing out various landmarks around the Bay and in the city centre sprawling below them.

More and more lights came on as they watched, and then finally the sun sank into the sea, the sky darkening to ink as night enveloped the landscape, broken only by pinpricks of light in the velvet blackness.

She shivered, and he wrapped his arms around her and rested his chin on her head, pulling her back firmly against his chest so she could feel his powerful body reassuringly solid behind her.

'Thank you for bringing me here,' she said softly. 'It's lovely. I haven't been away for so long.'

'When?' he asked. 'When was the last time you went away for a night?'

She shook her head, feeling the rasp of his chin against her hair. 'I don't know. Years. When Stephen was small. Roger and I went to London to a show. Five years ago?'

His arms tightened. 'You need spoiling,' he murmured. 'I'll leave you to unpack and change, then we can go and have a drink before dinner. How long do you want? Do you need to lie down for a while?'

She laughed softly, guilt prickling her. 'Hardly. I'm afraid I dozed in the car. So much for sharing the driving.'

'You were tired. What time were you up?'

'Four,' she confessed. 'I remembered there weren't enough tray bakes.'

He sighed into her hair. 'You work too hard. So what do you want? An hour?'

'Half an hour? How dressy is dinner?'

'Not very. Smart casual.'

She grimaced. She wasn't sure she could do smart casual, but she'd brought the dress. He'd seemed to like it on Tuesday, at least, and let's face it, her choices were distinctly limited! She could dress it up with her only bits of jewellery and the lovely soft cream pashmina the girls had given her for Christmas.

'I'll book us a table for eight, shall I? That'll give you half an hour to get ready and an hour for us to unwind and look at the menu.'

She nodded. 'Sounds good.'

He brushed a kiss on her cheek, and she felt his stubble graze her skin lightly, leaving it tingling.

'See you soon,' he murmured.

He went out, and she looked around at the huge room. It seemed much too big just for her, and she found herself wishing she was sharing it with him.

Still, at least he was treating her with respect. Any other man would have expected her to sleep with him if he'd gone to all this trouble and expense. She should be grateful.

But she wasn't grateful. She was lonely, and tingling with anticipation, and she was more than ready for the next step.

He contemplated a tie, but it was so long since he'd worn one he thought it would strangle him.

Damn. Was it necessary?

No. It was a Savile Row shirt, one of his favourites, and with his navy chinos and a linen jacket he was sure he'd do. But then he thought of Annie, of what she'd be doing now. Hair, make-up, those ridiculous little shoes that were all pointy toes and heels so high she'd need oxygen. And that dress? Please, God, let her wear the dress—

He put on the tie, checked his watch and tapped on her door.

'Coming!' she called, and after a few seconds the door swung in.

He nearly punched the air.

She was wearing the dress, and she looked if anything

even more stunning than she had the other night. And she smelt of—oh, God help him, she was wearing that perfume. The perfume she'd worn in France, the perfume that had haunted him for years.

He sucked in a slow, measured breath, took a step back and groped around for a smile.

'All set?' he said, his voice sounding even more strained than usual, and she nodded.

'I'll just get my things.'

She disappeared for a second, coming back with her bag in one hand and a cream shawl thing in the other. 'Do you think I'll need this?'

He shrugged. 'I don't know. Bring it. You don't want to be cold.'

He knew it wouldn't be a problem for him. Just looking at her was putting him in danger of spontaneous combustion. They went up to the bar, and he turned to her and raised a brow.

'Fancy champagne? To celebrate escaping?'

She hesitated, then that soft, lovely smile lit up her eyes. 'What a good idea. Thank you.'

So they started with champagne—just a half bottle, because they would have something different with their meal—and he lifted his glass and met her eyes.

'To you—for being the most special woman I've ever met. One of the bravest, kindest, least selfish people it's ever been my privilege to know. And to us.'

She swallowed, her eyes sparkling, and lifted her glass. 'To us,' she said, her voice thready with emotion. A tear shimmered on her lashes, then slid down her cheek, and he reached out and caught it with his thumb, sweeping it gently away.

'I love you,' he said gruffly.

She looked down. 'Oh, Michael,' she began, but then the waitress came to take their order, and the moment was lost.

He didn't mind. There'd be others, and he'd rather hear the words when she knew who she was saying them to. His jaw clenched. He was dreading telling her, but he'd have to do it soon. Tomorrow night?

Not tonight, because they were trapped together, and she'd probably need time to get used to the idea, and if she wanted to get away from him it would be somewhat difficult with two kids in the car and a two hundred and fifty mile trip to get through.

So, tomorrow night, then.

And God help him.

The meal was wonderful.

Elegantly presented, cooked to perfection, the flavours a perfect complement to each other.

All of this she noted, the cook in her taking an academic interest. The rest of her, the woman who was slowly coming to terms with the fact that she'd fallen headlong in love with the man sharing this experience with her, wouldn't have cared if they'd been in a greasy spoon eating beans on toast.

So long as she'd been with him.

They laughed, they argued about education and politics and advertising, and all the time all she could think about was being alone with him.

Holding him in her arms. Loving him. Him loving her.

'Was everything all right for you?'

Michael glanced up, smiled distractedly at the waitress and nodded.

'Wonderful. Thank you. Can we have our coffee by the fire?'

'Of course, sir. I'll bring it through to you. Any drinks?'

'Want a liqueur?' he asked her, but she shook her head.

'I've had enough.' Any more and she was likely to disgrace herself. Her inhibitions were well out of the window anyway.

'Just the coffee, thank you,' he said, getting to his feet and helping her out of the chair, then placing a warm, proprietorial hand on the small of her back and ushering her through to the lounge.

They sat by the window again, so they could see the flames licking through the logs on the fire and the lights stretched out below them, twinkling in the distance.

'All right?'

She nodded. 'Wonderful. Never better.'

'Good.'

His smile was tender, but there was a burning intensity about him that made the breath catch in her lungs.

Suddenly she didn't want the coffee. She just wanted to be alone with him. But it was here now, and he was pouring it and handing her a cup, so she drank it; nibbled one of the sinful little chocolates and wished she knew how to tell him what she was feeling.

'You look tired,' he said suddenly, and put his cup down. 'Come on. Let's call it a day.'

She nodded, got to her feet, walked down to their rooms with her heart in her mouth because she was going to ask him—

'Key?'

She fumbled in her bag, handed him the card, and he slid it into the slot, turned the handle and gave her back the key.

'Are you coming in?' she asked, holding her breath for his reply, but he shook his head.

'No.' He swallowed, his Adam's apple working. 'Don't tempt me, Annie,' he said, his voice low and rough with desire, making her body ache. 'It's difficult enough to be a gentleman. I'll see you in the morning.'

He brushed her lips with his, backing away and closing her door before she could reach for him, and she turned and slumped against the door. She could have screamed with frustration.

'Goodnight, my love,' he murmured through the door, then she heard his door open and close, and she shut her eyes and dropped her head forwards and sighed.

So much for her night of passion.

He stood in the shower under the pounding spray for what seemed like hours. He didn't believe in cold showers. They were just unpleasant and only worked for a few minutes. So the water was hot, and so was he, but at least the tension was gone from his neck and shoulders and he was squeaky clean.

He sluiced the water from his face and hair, grabbed a towel and rubbed himself roughly dry, then put on the towelling robe from the back of the door and went out into the bedroom.

The bed mocked him, acres of it lonely and empty and taunting. When he'd come down with Ruth to research the book set in Cardiff and the Brecon Beacons, he'd imagined bringing Annie here.

Making love to her on just such a bed, in the room next door, where she was lying now.

The result had been the hottest, most passionate and emotional ending he'd ever written. Ruth had cried. Ruth, who never showed any emotion, had cried.

So had he.

And he could cry right now, with frustration.

'One more day. That's all. Just one more day. Hang in there.'

He lay in bed staring at the ceiling, then forced himself to relax. He'd got to drive tomorrow. Make that today. It must be after midnight. He didn't want to crash and kill them all when he'd come this far.

He slowed his breathing, his heartrate, consciously tensed and relaxed each muscle group, and gradually he dozed off.

A noise woke him, just a slight click, but after all the years of training it was enough. Senses on full alert, he opened his eyes a crack and checked the room.

Nothing.

He eased out of bed and padded silently to the French doors. The noise had been outside—Annie's door opening?

And then he saw her, huddled in the hotel's towelling robe, staring out over the twinkling lights. He opened his door and went out, and she turned to him and smiled ruefully.

'I'm sorry—did I wake you?' she said softly.

'I wasn't really asleep,' he admitted.

She walked up to him, placed her hand on his heart, looked up into his eyes.

'Nor was I. I couldn't sleep without you,' she said, and he groaned and closed his eyes.

'Annie, no. We can't do this—'

'Why?'

'It's too soon.'

She gave a funny, brittle little laugh. 'It doesn't feel too soon, believe me.'

He took her hand in his, gripping it like a lifeline. 'We need to talk. There are things you don't know about me—'

'Are you married?'

He shook his head. 'No—'

'No mystery woman stashed away somewhere?'

'Only you.' Only ever you, for so, so long—

'Can I trust you?'

'Absolutely.'

'Then that's all I need to know.' She swallowed, and he realised she was nervous. Her eyes, though, locked with his, and he could see all the way down to her soul. 'I need you, Michael,' she whispered. 'Make love to me—please.'

Dear God forgive him, he wasn't strong enough—

With a shattered groan he hauled her up against his chest, slanted his mouth over hers and kissed her as if his life depended on it. When he came up for air he couldn't speak, couldn't think, couldn't do anything except scoop her up in his arms, kick her door open and then closed behind them and then lay her on the huge, soft bed and follow her down.

Her robe parted, giving him access to the warm satin skin that he'd longed to touch. His mouth raided it, plundering her body, touching it all—her breasts, full and soft and achingly aroused, her waist, slender and neat, the smooth, taut bowl of her abdomen, the fine, tender skin of her inner thigh—then finally, the most intimate caress of all.

She came apart under his touch, tugging at him wildly, his hair, his robe, pulling him up her, taking his face in her hands and kissing him as the tears poured down her cheeks and the climax tore through her.

'Please—now!' she begged, and he buried himself in her sweet, welcoming body and gave in to the passion that had ridden him for nine long, endless years.

'Annie!' he groaned, then arching up, he felt a great cry rip through him as his body slammed against hers for the final time, the sensation too much as she convulsed around him, her own cry lost in the echo of his as he spilt deep inside her.

As the echoes died away, he felt her body go limp against him, cradling him in its softness. 'Michael,' she whispered raggedly. 'Oh, Michael—'

He dropped his head into the hollow of her shoulder and struggled for air. 'I love you,' he said.

'I know, my darling,' she murmured, her voice unsteady, her hands stroking him tenderly—tenderly enough to bring tears to his eyes. 'I love you, too.'

Her arms tightened around him as he tried to shift his weight from her, so he eased to his side, taking her with him, and collapsed against the pillows, cradling her against his chest.

She fell asleep almost instantly, but he lay awake, berating himself for his weakness, cursing his stupidity, his lack of self-control.

He should have told her before he'd allowed this to happen. It was wrong. So many lies.

'Forgive me, my love,' he whispered soundlessly. 'Please forgive me…'

She woke to the sound of his heartbeat under her ear, one leg wedged between his solid, hair-roughened thighs and her hand enfolded in his.

His other hand curled protectively over her back, the fingers splayed across her ribs. She moved a fraction, and his eyes flew open and locked with hers.

'Good morning,' she said softly, and he searched her eyes, his face expressionless.

'Good morning.'

His voice was gruff and sleep-roughened, rasping like sandpaper across her senses. And, talking of sandpaper, she lifted her hand and rubbed her palm sensuously over his jaw, revelling in the coarse and very male drag of stubble on her skin.

'Mmm,' she groaned softly, and he rocked against her, tipping her on to her back and following her over, plundering her mouth as his hands explored her body lazily. He lifted his head and stared down at her, his face no longer expressionless, and she felt the surge of passion in his body. Heat coiled through her, and she threaded her fingers through his hair, drew his face down to hers again and took his mouth in a kiss full of promise.

Later, when she'd recovered her breath and her heartbeat had slowed, she smiled up at him and stroked his jaw with her fingertips.

'Wow,' she murmured. 'You can wake me up like that every morning for the rest of my life if you like.'

A shadow seemed to flit through his eyes, leaving them troubled. 'I hope you'll give me that chance,' he said quietly. He glanced at his watch, then sighed. 'Annie, we have to make a move. The wind's picking up—if it gets much worse they'll close the Severn Bridge and we'll have to go the long way round, and we've got far enough to go as it is.'

He was pulling away from her, not just physically but emotionally. She could feel it, feel the chill of his withdrawal, and she felt curiously afraid.

'Michael—you said you wanted to talk,' she said, suddenly realising that she needed to know whatever it was. Needed to know it now—

'Later. Not now. I want time alone with you. Tonight?'

'I'll have Stephen, but that's not a problem. We can talk after he's gone to bed. He won't be late. If they've been up all night he'll be out like a light by eight.'

He nodded. 'OK.'

He stood up, pulling his gown back around him and tugging the belt tight. 'I'll see you in half an hour for breakfast.'

And with that he went out on to the terrace, closed her door behind him and she heard his door click shut seconds later.

A shiver went over her, and she frowned.

Whatever he had to say to her, it couldn't be that bad. Could it?

He dropped her off at her house at three and headed home. There were things he wanted to gather together before their talk—things he had to show her. And he needed time to get his head in order.

First, though, was a nice long soak in the hot tub to ease out the kinks of the drive. The tension of these last few weeks was killing him, and he could feel a headache starting up, not helped by Stephen and Ed who'd been chattering non-stop in the car the entire way. Oh, well, at least they seemed to have had a good time.

He put the kettle on, took a long, ice-cold drink of water from the fridge dispenser and downed some pills, then stared out over the valley towards her house.

The wind was picking up, bending the trees, the gusts growing stronger by the minute.

Gales had been forecast, and it seemed they weren't wrong. He'd thought it was rough on the way back, the crosswind tugging at the car. The bridge had been open early in the morning, but he'd lay odds it was closed now.

He felt a prickle in the back of his neck, and he frowned.

It was his early-warning system, and he absolutely never ignored it. It had saved his life more times than he cared to remember. His eyes flicked to Annie's house, and the prickling got worse.

Damn.

He was just reaching for the phone when it rang, and he grabbed it.

'Harding.'

Her voice was frantic. 'Michael, it's Annie—Stephen's gone up the beech tree after the cat, and the tree's creaking and now he's stuck and I don't know what to do and I'm so scared it's going to fall—'

His gut clenched with fear. The beech tree was huge—!

'I'm coming. Tell him to stay still. Keep out of the way of the tree, do you understand?' He said it again for emphasis. 'Keep out of the way of the tree. Tell him to stay where he is. I'll be with you in five minutes.'

It took him three, and he nearly put the Aston in the ditch on the S-bend, but then he was there and running into the back garden.

'Where is he?'

'There—' She pointed up into the tree and then he saw him, clinging to a branch, his face white with terror. It was an old tree, and beeches weren't known for their longevity. The roots were probably rotten, and it was creaking ominously with every gust.

If he was lucky, he'd got minutes.

'Michael, get him down, please—!'

'Don't worry. Get back out of the way, Annie. I'll get him.'

There was an old rope ladder at the bottom, attached to one of the lower branches, and he shinned up it in no time flat.

'Don't worry, Stephen, I'm coming,' he yelled over the noise of the wind. 'Hang on tight.'

'The cat,' he sobbed, and Michael glanced across to the end of the branch his son was clinging on to and saw the frightened ginger tom hanging on for dear life. He wasn't alone. As Michael got to him, he could see Stephen's knuckles were white and the boy was shaking.

'It's OK, son, I've got you,' he said, grabbing hold of

his jumper with an iron fist. 'Right. I want you to turn and wrap your arms around my neck. Slowly, now. That's it. Good boy. Now your legs round my waist, and hang on tight.'

'What about Tigger?'

'I can't reach Tigger. Let me get you down first.'

'But you must—'

'In a minute. Hang on, we're going down.'

He glanced down and saw Annie standing, her fists pressed to her mouth, eyes wide with terror.

The wind gusted again, nearly tearing him from the trunk, but he leant into it and hung on as the huge old tree shifted and groaned. He could feel it going, but then the wind eased and he reached out his foot, groping for a branch.

'Left a bit,' Annie called, and he found the branch, swung down to the ladder and slithered down it to the ground.

'You have to get Tigger!' Stephen was sobbing.

'Michael, no!'

'It's OK. Go to your mum, Stephen. I'll get him.'

His son slid from his arms and ran towards Annie, and as Michael turned to go back up for the cat, cursing himself for a fool, the wind gusted again, there was an ominous crack and as if in slow motion the huge tree started to topple towards him.

'*Run!*' he bellowed and, turning on his heel, he sprinted towards them, throwing himself over them as the tree crashed down around them.

He felt a stabbing pain in his leg, then there was another crack as the branches whiplashed in the aftermath, his head felt as if it had been split open and everything went black…

CHAPTER NINE

'MRS HARDING?'

She opened her mouth to explain that she wasn't Michael's wife, but then shut it and stood up, going towards the doctor.

'How is he?'

'Dazed, disorientated, nauseous—he's had quite a blow to the head, but we're rather concerned, in view of the extent of his previous surgery.'

'Concerned?' she echoed. 'He's not going to—?'

She broke off, unable to say the words, but the doctor shook her head. 'Not unless something changes radically, but we will need to keep him in overnight to be on the safe side. He keeps talking about Stephen, asking if he's all right, and he's asking for you—I take it you're Annie?'

'I am.' She nodded. 'Can I see him?'

'Of course. Come with me.'

She led Annie from the all too familiar relatives' room through into another place that was every bit as familiar. Resus. She'd been here several times with Roger over the years, and the place gave her the creeps.

Michael was lying on a trolley-type bed, wired up to monitors that bleeped and squeaked and frightened the living daylights out of her.

Oh, Lord. Not Michael, too, she prayed. Please, not Michael, too. I can't lose another person that I love—

'Annie?'

His voice was rough and scratchy, but his eyes were wide open and locked on to hers like a laser, and she went straight to his side and took his hand, hanging on like grim death.

'Michael! I was so worried. Are you OK?'

'I'm fine,' he said dismissively. 'What about Stephen?'

'He's OK. He's shaken up and scared, but he's with Ed's parents. They're keeping him overnight. He's got a few bumps and scratches, but he's all right.'

'What about you?'

'I'm fine. We both are.'

'You sure?'

His voice was slurred, but the urgency was all too clear and she hurried to reassure him.

'I'm sure. I wouldn't lie to you.'

His eyes closed briefly. 'Going to be sick,' he said, and turning his head, he retched helplessly.

She reached out a hand and smoothed back his hair, tears coursing unheeded down her cheeks. The nurse dealt with the bowl, wiped his mouth and settled him back on the blood-soaked pillow while she just stood there and tried not to fall apart.

'Don't worry about the blood,' the doctor said, leading her to one side. 'He's got a head wound, they always bleed a lot. We've glued it already, and it's the least of our concerns. I've asked the maxillo-facial surgeon to come down and take a look at his X-rays, because frankly I'm out of my depth. I just wondered if you could tell me where he had his facial reconstruction done, so we can speak to the surgeons there and get any information we might need to read the X-rays.'

'Reconstruction?' she murmured. 'I'm sorry, I don't know. We haven't been together all that long.' Try two weeks— 'Ruth might know.'

'Ruth?'

'A friend—I've called her, she should be here soon.'

'Got one for me?' a man asked, and the doctor left her side and flicked a switch, bringing up the light behind a set of X-rays that even Annie could see weren't normal.

She frowned at them. Good grief. She'd realised he'd had an injury, obviously, but that extensive? There seemed to be bits of metal everywhere!

The newcomer was pointing out things on the plates, and Annie could catch the odd word, but not all of them.

'Replaced cheekbones—massive dental work—jaw—orbit must be altered—sight affected—contact lenses or glasses?'

'Contact lenses.'

She blinked at Michael. She'd never realised he wore contact lenses, and she'd certainly never seen him in glasses.

'Amazing work,' the man was saying, shaking his head and turning to look at Michael so she could hear him more clearly. 'Fantastic result, you really wouldn't know to look at him—must have been a hell of an injury. I would say he was lucky to survive, but he probably didn't think so at the time. I doubt if his own mother would recognise him now. Let's have a word.'

He went over to Michael, bent over him and smiled. 'Hi there. I'm Mr Hughes, the maxillo-facial surgeon. I've been called in to have a look at your X-rays. Can you tell me your name?'

'Michael—Harding.'

'OK. Can you tell me about your accident?'

'Tree fell on me.'

'OK, Mr Harding. What about before—when your face was damaged?'

'Armstrong,' he mumbled. 'It's Armstrong…'

Annie blinked. Armstrong? *Armstrong?*

The doctors exchanged significant glances.

But he was slurring more and more, starting to ramble, and Mr Hughes fished out a penlight and flashed in it his eyes. That didn't go down well and Michael turned away with a groan and retched again.

'OK, I think you need to keep an eye on him but his pupils are equal and reactive. I can't see any obvious fractures but I'd like a chat with him when he's feeling better, to make sure there's nothing unforeseen going on. And check the neck again. It might just be whiplash—it's typical of severe facial injuries. Anything that hits the face that hard affects the neck, and the effects can be long-lasting and recurrent. Keep an eye out for a head injury; he's obviously confused, but he's very photophobic. He might be suffering from nothing more than migraine. Has he had pain relief?'

The doctor shook her head. 'Not yet.'

'I would give him morphine—'

'Not morphine,' Michael mumbled. 'Not again. Not going cold turkey again, please. OK now. Just turn off the lights...'

He trailed off, and they dimmed the lights around him slightly and he seemed to relax a little.

'Mrs Harding?' a nurse was saying. 'I've got all his things here that were in his pockets. As we're going to admit him I've got to list them and ask you to sign for them.'

'Of course,' she said, thinking that she really must tell them that she wasn't Mrs Harding—or Mrs Armstrong, come to that. What was that about? Funny thing to get confused about—

'There's just a few things—his phone, his keys, his wallet—that's got £26.58 in it, and three cards, and this ring and chain and a photo—'

'That's my grandmother's ring,' she said, feeling a cold

shiver run over her. She reached for it and picked it up, staring down at it in confusion. Why did Michael have it? She'd given it to Etienne—

'Tell me where he had his facial reconstruction done—you really wouldn't know to look at him—fantastic result—I doubt if his own mother would recognise him now...'

Or his lover?

She felt the blood drain from her face.

Etienne. He was Etienne.

Or Michael Harding.

Or Michael Armstrong?

She backed away. 'I—I'm sorry, I need some air.'

She turned and ran out, past the nurses, through the double doors and out into the car park, dragging in great lungfuls of air and gulping down the nausea.

Who was he?

'Annie?'

She looked up into Ruth's pale and worried face.

'Who is he?' she asked in a strange, hollow voice that she didn't recognise. 'I don't know who he is, Ruth—what his name is, even. What's going on?'

Ruth swore softly under her breath. 'I knew this would happen. Where is he?'

She swallowed. 'Resus. He's OK. He's got a head injury—they did X-rays—called a specialist down. He'd never seen anything like it—'

She turned away, bile rising in her throat, and felt Ruth's hand on her shoulder.

'Idiot. I told him to tell you—'

'Tell me what, Ruth? What is it he has to tell me? And how much do you know about it?'

Ruth was silent, but her face said it all.

Annie backed away, shaking her head. 'You know, don't you? You know all about it—you always have, right from the beginning. He said you go back years—how many years, Ruth? Nine? Is it nine?'

Ruth's eyes filled with tears. 'Don't hate him, Annie. He loves you.'

'Does he? Which one of him? Etienne Duprés? Michael Harding? Or Michael Armstrong, whoever the hell he might be? I haven't been introduced to that one yet—'

She turned, walking away from the hospital, her legs moving faster and faster until she was running, fighting against the wind that was tugging at her hair and streaking the tears as they fell down her cheeks.

Hands stopped her. Big, gentle hands that halted her progress and turned her, sobbing, against a firm, hard chest.

'Do you want me to take you home?'

She looked up, scanned an unfamiliar but kindly face with worried eyes.

'I'm Tim Warren, by the way. Ruth's fiancé.'

The policeman. Surely he would be all right? She nodded. 'If you don't mind. I don't think I can take any more—'

'Let me tell Ruth what we're doing. Hang on.'

He ran back to her, spoke briefly, kissed her cheek and then was back by Annie's side, his hand under her elbow, guiding her towards his car.

Twenty minutes later she was home, and she held herself together just long enough to close the door on Tim before the dam burst.

She lifted her hand to her mouth to hold back the sobs, and realised she was still holding the ring—the ring she'd given Etienne nine years ago on that fateful night to keep him safe.

But what about her? What about keeping her safe, because nothing now seemed to make any sense.

'*Who are you?*' she whispered. '*What do you want with me? What do you want with my son?*'

'Idiot.'

Michael winced. 'Don't. Head hurts.'

'Good. It's no more than you deserve,' Ruth ranted at him, then turned away, talking to someone else. The doctor? 'Is he going to be all right?'

'I believe so. Where's Mrs Harding gone? I wanted to ask her something.'

'Home,' Ruth said, and he lay there puzzled and tried to work out who she was talking about. There *was* no Mrs Harding—and why was Ruth saying it was no more than he deserved? He'd been saving Stephen—

'She wasn't feeling well,' Ruth was saying. 'I think she's gone to check on their son. Is it OK if I stay with him?'

'Only if you don't nag,' he slurred, still trying to work it out.

'You wish. I'm his sister,' she lied, and glared down at him.

He grunted, glaring back at her. 'Where's Annie gone?' he mumbled.

'Home. She knows, Michael.'

It took a second to register, then his eyes slid shut and he swore, softly but fluently, in French.

'Go after her.'

'Tim's with her. He's taking her home.'

'Good idea,' he mumbled. 'Going home. Want to go home.'

'Sorry, we have to keep you in,' the doctor said. 'I need to monitor you—'

Pretty little thing. Couldn't have been more than about twelve. He tried to smile at her, but his mouth wouldn't work.

'You'll have to duct-tape me to the trolley,' he mumbled. 'I'm going. Get me the forms.'

'Mr Harding, it really isn't a good idea—'

He sat up and swayed, glaring at the cot sides. 'Let me out of here,' he said firmly and much more clearly. 'I know the risks. I don't have a head injury—I've got a migraine. Got pills at home. Going home—Ruth, get me out. Oh, hell, sick again—'

He retched into a bowl shoved under his face in the nick of time by the long-suffering doctor, and glowered at her defiantly. 'Just let me go.'

'I can't. Why don't you lie down and—?'

'Because I'm going home,' he said clearly. 'Either with or without your approval.' His gaze swivelled to Ruth. 'Where's your car?'

'I'm in Tim's—and he's taking Annie back. Stay till tomorrow, Michael, be reasonable.'

But he couldn't, because he had to get out of here and talk to Annie—and he couldn't do that pinned out like a butterfly and wired up to God knows what. And anyway, he didn't trust them not to pump him full of morphine, and he'd had enough of that to last him a lifetime.

'Now, Ruth,' he pleaded. 'Get me a taxi. Get me out of here.'

Annie didn't know what to do.

All she knew was that she was afraid. She didn't know who he was, or what he wanted, but she knew—she just *knew*—that he was in some way involved with Claude Gaultier.

And that scared the life out of her.

And Ruth? She was involved, too, but she was marrying a policeman. Did that make her one of the good guys? And what about Michael? Was he a good guy or a bad guy?

And how could she tell? Oh, God, how had she got herself *involved* in this?

And then she thought of Stephen, and her fear escalated. Michael had been around for years, lurking in the background, somehow contriving to own her tearoom, with Ruth installed in the flat overhead monitoring every detail of their lives.

Befriending her. Spying on her, for heaven's sake! And on Stephen—babysitting him, of all things. And she'd told them in words of one syllable that Stephen was his son. Etienne's son. Michael's son.

The same thing.

Except Etienne had been a playboy, a charmer, a gentleman in his rather light-hearted way. She'd never taken him seriously, but she'd loved him anyway.

But Michael. What kind of man was Michael?

More to the point, *who* was Michael?

What did he want with them? Was he working for Gaultier? Surely not. Gaultier had been killed—unless he wasn't the real boss? But why would any of them be interested in her? What did she know that meant she had to be stalked for nine years? Or was he just after Stephen?

She closed her eyes, breathing deeply to quell the panic. She could feel the wind shaking the house, rattling the glass in the windows. There was a draught under the study door, and she went in there to see if the sash had slipped with the howling gale and something crunched under her shoes.

She flicked on the light and stared in horror. The window had gone, the glass exploded all across the floor, and the hole where it had been was filled with broken branches. One of the bookcases had been knocked over, and Michael's book, the one set in Wales, lay open on the floor at the title page, signed with his bold scrawl.

For Roger, with every good wish, Michael.

He'd been here, met Roger. Infiltrated her family when she'd been out—with Ruth's help? How many times had he been here while they'd been out? How many times had he seen Stephen? With every good wish? She didn't think so. She didn't think so at all, but then she didn't know what to think.

She lifted the phone, staring at the mess, not knowing whether to cry or run. Who could she phone? The police?

Why? They'd ask her questions she had no answers to. The only person who had the answers was Michael, and she had no intention of asking him anything.

She cradled the phone, picked it up again and called Grace.

'Help me,' she said, her body shaking. 'I'm so scared—'

'Annie? My God, what's happened? Where are you?'

'Home. The tree fell down. Michael's in hospital, but it isn't that. He isn't—'

'I'll be right there.'

The line went dead, and she clutched the receiver until the message to please hang up and try again finally penetrated her daze. She put it down and stared at it.

She thought of calling the girls, but what was the point of worrying them? Surely they were safe? Unless he was part of the human trafficking thing?

No. She knew he wasn't. The way he'd made love to her—nobody involved in trafficking prostitutes could be so gentle, so passionate—could they?

'Annie? Annie, open the damn door!'

She opened it, and Grace swept in and hugged her tight.

'Sweetheart, tell me all. What's happened?'

She didn't know where to start, so she began with the

most important thing, the thing that somehow drifted to the top.

'He's Stephen's father,' she said.

Grace stared at her. 'But—he's dead.'

'No. He's Michael—but I didn't know. His face is different—his voice. His injuries—'

She remembered the X-rays, and shuddered. What must he have gone through? No. Don't think about that. Don't let yourself feel sorry for him. Not until you know—

'Annie? Annie, let me in, I need to talk to you.'

The knocking on the door was relentless, insistent, and they turned towards it uncertainly.

'Ruth,' she said, looking at Grace with fear. 'I don't know if I can trust her. She knew all about it—'

'I'll get it,' Grace said firmly and, pushing past her, she opened the door. 'What is it?'

'I want to see Annie.'

'Maybe she doesn't want to see you.'

'Please, Grace. I need to talk to her—to explain.'

Grace snorted. 'It had better be good—and who are you?'

She heard a low murmur, and Grace stood back. 'OK. You'd better not be a bad cop. I'm a journalist.'

'I'm not a bad cop,' Tim said firmly, pocketing his ID, and following Ruth in; he closed the door and met Annie's eyes. 'Annie, please listen to Ruth. At least hear what she has to say.'

She swallowed hard and nodded. 'All right—but just five minutes.'

'Where's Stephen?' Ruth asked.

'Somewhere safe,' she replied, not even questioning her choice of words.

'Good. He doesn't need to hear this. Tim, could you take a look outside at the tree and make sure the house is OK?'

Annie laughed raggedly. 'I should start in the study. Half of it's in there.'

She turned away, going through to the kitchen, retreating automatically to the room where she felt safe. 'OK, fire away.'

Ruth glanced at Grace. 'Could we have a minute?'

Grace hesitated, then nodded. 'I'll be just outside,' she promised, and closed the door.

'May I sit down?'

Annie nodded, then pulled out a chair and sat down herself. Quickly, before she fell. 'OK, start talking. Who is he? Why is he spying on me? And why are you spying on me? For umpteen bloody years, pretending to be my friend, coming into my home, babysitting my child. How could you, Ruth?'

'Because he asked me to keep an eye on you, to make sure you were safe and that everything was all right.'

'It was—until he came along!'

'That's not fair.'

'How do I know that? I don't even know who he is—and, as for keeping me safe, I've never been so terrified in my life! Ruth, what the hell is going on? Who is he—and come to that, who are you?'

'Me? I'm who I am. You know me.'

'I don't think so. And Michael? What's your connection with Michael? Is that his name, by the way?'

Ruth sighed, and started talking. 'His name's Michael Armstrong. He was in military intelligence. When you met him, he and David were working undercover, trying to get evidence on Claude Gaultier, the owner—'

'I know who Gaultier is. It's Michael I'm having a problem with—and your connection to him. And who's David?'

'You knew him as Gerard.'

'The man who died?'

Ruth nodded, and something that could have been pain flashed in her eyes and was gone. 'David and I were lovers. We were in the police together, in immigration. He was seconded to the task force to work with Michael, because he was bilingual. I was working in London, with the prostitutes. I was—raped. I was in hospital when it all went wrong in France. The first I heard, David was dead, and Michael had survived. Just. They stuck him back together again, gave him a new identity and sent him into the military equivalent of retirement under witness protection.'

No wonder she'd been unable to get anything out of the police in France. They must have been hushed up in a big way. And Ruth's David had been Gerard, the dead man. And she'd been raped. Poor Ruth. No. Don't feel sorry for her, she's in this up to her lying little neck, she told herself. But that didn't explain everything anyway, not by a long chalk. Not the years after that night.

'So why did he come here?' she asked, refusing to back down because she *needed* these answers. 'Why did he buy the Ancient House, and live so close, and put you in the flat? Don't tell me it was coincidence.'

She shook her head. 'Oh, no. It was quite deliberate. And he had to pull some pretty impressive strings to be allowed to be here and work with me while we watched you. I still don't know how he did it, or why he bothered with me.'

'But why did he want to be near me? Was it just because of Stephen?'

'You'll have to ask him that. I've told you all I can—all that's mine to tell. All I know, really—except that he would die for you and his son.'

That was true. He'd nearly died that afternoon, throwing himself over them to protect them from the falling tree, shielding them with his body, and the horror of that moment would be with her for ever. But that didn't explain his secrecy.

'Why didn't he tell me who he was?'

'He couldn't. He's bound by the Official Secrets Act. So am I. As long as the case was ongoing, there was nothing he could do. Until Gaultier was arrested.'

'But it all came to a head just over two weeks ago,' Annie said slowly. 'That's when you moved out—when he came into my life.'

'Because he could, at last.'

'And yet still he didn't tell me who he was,' she said, still puzzled. 'Why didn't he, Ruth? Why didn't he tell me then who he was? Was he trying to gather evidence for custody or something?'

Ruth looked horrified. 'No! Nothing like that, I promise you.'

'So what, then?'

She shook her head. 'You'll have to ask him that. I told him to, warned him. He had some crazy idea about getting to know you from scratch. Go and talk to him, Annie. He's a good man. The best. He's only ever had your safety and happiness at heart.'

'And Stephen's? What about Stephen?'

Her face softened. 'He adores Stephen. It's killed him having to watch him from a distance.'

'But—he couldn't have known he was his son. Not for certain. Not until I told him.'

Ruth looked away, and Annie felt the icy chill of betrayal. 'How did he know?' she asked, her voice cold.

'DNA,' Ruth confessed. 'I cut a little bit of his hair one night when I babysat for you.'

She stood up, backing away from the woman she'd thought was her friend. Her legs were shaking, and her voice wasn't her own, but she couldn't take any more. She just wanted Ruth out, wanted this to be over.

'OK, that's enough. I want you to go.'

'Annie, talk to him. Give him a chance to explain.'

'I don't know that he can. He might be a national hero, Ruth, but he's lied to me, deceived me, cheated his way into my life, my bed, my heart—and I don't think I can ever forgive him for that, whatever his motivation.'

'And me?' Ruth asked, lifting her head and meeting Annie's eyes, her own tortured. 'Can you forgive me?'

She couldn't speak. Instead, she simply turned away, and after a moment the door closed softly and left her in silence—a silence broken only by the sound of her own weeping.

CHAPTER TEN

THE next hours and days were hell. Afterwards, Annie didn't know how she'd got through them, but somehow she did.

Tim was wonderful. He took Ruth back to Michael's, then returned with a saw and a hammer and some nails and dealt with the tree, weatherproofing the house with tacked-on plastic sheeting and some old boards as a temporary measure until the morning.

He didn't say much, and Annie was grateful for that. He just worked quietly and steadily, securing her home, clearing up the broken glass in the study, righting the bookcase and returning the books to it.

At least the wind had died down, so the plastic sheet was secure enough to weatherproof it, but the boards across it wouldn't have held back a determined intruder, and Annie was afraid.

'Do you want me to stay?' he asked, but she shook her head.

'No. I'm being silly. I'll be all right. It's Michael I'm afraid of, and he's too ill to be a threat at the moment.'

He hesitated, then said, very gently, 'Michael won't hurt you, Annie. He saved Ruth's life. She tried to kill herself a few months after David died. He wouldn't let her. He kept her going, looked after her, made her feel safe. Without him she wouldn't be here now, and nor would a lot of other people. He's a good man. A really decent man, and he's been through hell. Give him a chance.'

166

He patted her shoulder awkwardly, then left her with Grace.

Grace, who hadn't left her side since Ruth had gone, who'd held her and let her cry and fed her tea and biscuits and refused to go home now.

'I'll stay with you.'

'I'll be all right.'

'Will you? I don't think so. You look like hell, Annie.'

She started to cry again. 'I just can't believe he didn't tell me. You know, Vicky was right. She said he was dangerous.'

'I don't think he is. You heard what Ruth said about him, what Tim just said.'

'But—military intelligence? Working undercover for the government? He must have killed people—that's what they do. Dog eat dog. I don't think I can spend my life with a ruthless killer, no matter why he did it.'

'But he's Stephen's father, Annie. Don't you think he has a right to see him, at least? That Stephen has a right to his father? They're wonderful together—you've seen them. And he might be a killer, but only because he had to, because someone has to do the dirty jobs to keep us all safe. That doesn't make him a bad person.'

But what Ruth had told her was still sinking in, and she couldn't think clearly. And until she could, until she could be sure that there was no threat whatsoever to her son, she had to keep him safe.

'I want to phone him.'

'Michael?'

'No! Stephen. I need to talk to him, make sure he's all right.'

He was, but he was very worried about Michael, and Annie had to struggle to reassure him. Even to say his name nearly choked her.

'He's gone home,' she told him. 'He's all right. He just had a little cut on his head.' And a face full of metal plates, and yet another name to add to the list—

'I want to see him.'

'I don't think that's a good idea. He's resting. You can see him next week, maybe. Look, Stephen, I want you to stay with Ed for a few days, OK? I'll drop some things over there for you in the morning.'

'But I want to come home.'

'The house is damaged,' she told him, sticking at least a little to the truth. 'Until it's mended you can't stay here. Your bedroom window's broken.'

Well, cracked, anyway, and the guttering was hanging. It was near enough, and it would have to do. Ed's mother had swallowed it, at least.

'I could sleep with you, in your room at the front,' he said, but she was adamant. She wasn't having him anywhere that Michael could find him—not until she was sure.

'Just stay there, darling. You like Ed—what's the problem?'

'I want to see Michael,' he said, and started crying. 'He's hurt, and it's my fault.'

'Nonsense. It's the cat's fault.'

'Is Tigger dead?'

She didn't know. She hadn't given the cat a moment's thought in all this, but Stephen needed to be reassured. And so she lied, cursing Michael for bringing her to this, making her lie to her son when she'd never lied to him in his life.

'No, he's fine,' she said, crossing her fingers and hoping it was true. She'd got enough to deal with without a dead cat. 'I'll see you in the morning—I'll pick you up and take you to school.'

Finally she prised him off the phone and went up to bed. She put Grace in Vicky's room, lent her a nightie and found her a fresh towel in the airing cupboard, then shut her bedroom door and stood there, not knowing quite what to do.

She didn't dare undress. Crazy, probably, but she didn't feel safe enough. Instead she unpacked her case, hanging up the dress she'd worn last night in Cardiff—so long ago. Lifetimes. She couldn't bear to think about it. He'd even toasted her, his eyes shining with sincerity.

'To you—for being the most special woman I've ever met. One of the bravest, kindest, least selfish people it's ever been my privilege to know. And to us.'

What us? Her and who, exactly? Some tough, ruthless undercover agent with a pretty line in lies? So much for his sincerity. She wrapped the pashmina around her shoulders and curled on to the chair by the window, wide, restless eyes watching the market square for signs of life.

There were none, but at about four in the morning she saw Tigger slinking nervously through the undergrowth in the front garden, and she went down and let him in. He was unscathed, and for once seemed pleased to see her.

'You have no idea what you've done,' she told him unsteadily, but the cat just rubbed himself against her legs and purred and then settled himself on the window sill and washed.

She made a pot of tea, thinking as she drained it that so much caffeine on top of all the drama probably wasn't good for her but not caring one way or the other. She had to do something, and sleep wasn't an option.

She checked the plastic over the window in the study, and it was fine, but her moving around disturbed Grace who came down and kept her company.

'What are you going to do?' she asked, and Annie shrugged.

'I don't know. I want to run away, but how can I? I've

got the girls to think about as well as Stephen, and the tearoom, and this house—I don't know where to start.'

'You could start by talking to Michael—in front of the police, if necessary, if that makes you feel safe? Or me. I'd come with you, if you want. Tim? Ruth? Maybe all of us.'

'And who can I trust, apart from you? I don't even know for sure about Tim. How do I really know he's a policeman?'

Grace sighed and sat back, hugging her knee to her chest. 'You have to start somewhere, Annie. You have to trust someone. I've seen his ID, but if you want proof phone the police—ask about him.'

She nodded, and reached for the phone book. 'I'll do it now.'

She did, and it seemed Tim was, indeed, a policeman. A detective inspector in the CID. A trawl on the internet revealed that DI Warren was very highly thought of. He had commendations for bravery, and he'd worked with victim support groups and on numerous rape cases.

And he thought Michael was a good man. Thought she should give him a chance.

She felt the threat recede a little, but the hurt and suspicion remained. She had to talk to Michael, she knew that, if only to thank him for saving Stephen's life.

Just not yet.

He had to see Michael. He knew there was something his mum wasn't telling him. She never lied, but she didn't always tell him everything. She hadn't when his dad was dying, and she had that same something odd in her voice, and he didn't know why.

He just knew he had to see Michael, to know he was alive and not badly hurt, because it had all been his fault and there was a sick lump in his chest that wouldn't go away.

So on Tuesday, when everyone went to lunch, he told Ed he was going to the loo and slipped out of the gate when the dinner lady wasn't looking and ran down the road.

He knew the way to the barn. Down the hill, over the bridge and through the wiggly bends, up the hill and then along the track to the right. But it was further than he'd thought, and it was raining, and he was cold and his legs were aching by the time he arrived.

He reached up and rang the doorbell, and nothing happened for ages. He must be dead, he was thinking, but then the door opened slowly and Michael stood there, staring down at him, and all he could do was cry.

He couldn't believe it. The kid was standing in the freezing rain, tears coursing down his cheeks, and fear ripped through him. He stooped and gathered the boy into his arms, and he burrowed into the space between Michael's neck and shoulder and whimpered, and the fear grew tenfold.

His arms tightened. 'What's wrong, Stephen? What's happened?'

'N-nothing,' he hiccuped. 'I thought you were dead. Mummy wouldn't let me see you, and I thought you must be dead—'

He felt tears in his own eyes, and blinked them savagely away, his hand finding and cradling the cold, wet head burrowing into him. 'It's all right, son. I'm fine. I just had a headache for a bit. Come on, let's get inside and tell your mum where you are.'

'She'll kill me,' he sobbed.

'No, she won't. She'll be worried, though. We don't

want her to worry. Why don't you go and dry off and I'll ring her? There's some towels in the wet room by the pool.'

He put the boy down, squeezed his shoulder for reassurance, and then as Stephen headed for the door, he picked up the phone and dialled her number.

She answered on the first ring. 'Stephen?' she said frantically, just as the sirens sounded outside his house.

'I've got him here,' he told her. 'He's—'

'What do you want with him?' she cried, her voice panic-stricken, pleading. 'You can have anything—I'll do anything, but please don't take him—'

He was stunned. 'Annie, I'm not taking him anywhere. What kind of a monster do you think I am? He just turned up, wringing wet and miserable—'

He glanced over his shoulder as the police burst in, and closed his eyes.

'He's through there,' he told them heavily, just as Stephen wandered back into the kitchen, rubbing his hair with a towel. 'Stephen, come and talk to your mother.'

He held out the phone, and the WPC took it and handed it to the boy, as if he couldn't be trusted to give him the receiver himself. She couldn't stop him looking at his son, though, and Stephen kept his eyes on Michael as he spoke, as if for moral support, and his lip started to wobble again.

'I'm sorry,' he said. 'I didn't mean to scare you, Mummy, but I thought Michael was dead, like Dad and my father, and I didn't want him to die too—'

Michael closed his eyes, squeezing them tight to hold back the tears. Poor little bastard. God, he loved him so much it hurt—

A hand landed on his shoulder.

'We'd like you to come down to the station with us, sir,' a voice said, and he turned and stared at the man in disbelief.

'I have done nothing wrong,' he said. 'Ask him. Ask the boy.'

He shook his head. 'Sorry, sir.'

'Ask DI Warren, then. He'll vouch for me.'

'We'll talk to him at the station.'

He resisted the urge to swear in front of the child, but there were some choice words running through his mind as he picked up his wallet and his keys.

'What about Stephen?'

'You let us worry about the boy, sir.'

'I'm not leaving him here with strangers. He's scared enough. When that tree fell—'

He looked across at his son, identical blue eyes meeting across the chaos, and Stephen ran to him.

He caught him in his arms, cradling him against his chest. 'I have to go, son,' he said gruffly. 'You'll be OK. Your mum'll be here in a minute.'

He heard the skid of tyres on gravel, and Annie ran through the door and stopped dead, staring at him.

For a long moment he met her eyes, reading distrust and fear and the soul-deep pain of betrayal, and knew he'd done this to her. He'd gambled, and he'd lost. When he allowed himself to think about it, the pain would kill him, but for now he had to go along with this farce.

He unwound Stephen's arms from his neck and handed him to his mother without a word, then turned back to the policeman who was waiting less than patiently.

'OK. Let's get this over with.'

'Why did the police want to talk to Michael, Mummy?'

Annie shook her head. 'I didn't know where you'd gone. I thought you might have gone there.' That he might have taken you, the most precious thing in my life—

'But why the police? Why didn't you just come and get me?'

She couldn't give him a proper answer, not without going into things she couldn't even begin to discuss with him, so she just hugged him again and said, 'I'm sorry. I over-reacted. I was just frightened for you.'

'But Michael wouldn't hurt me,' he said, puzzled. 'He likes me, I know he does.'

Such innocence. 'Just promise me you won't do it again,' she said, holding him at arm's length and looking searchingly at him. 'Promise.'

'I promise,' he mumbled. 'But I want to see him. He said I could swim and stuff.'

'He said that today?' Bribing him? She'd kill him—

'No. Last week. I told you.'

She relaxed a fraction. 'I'll think about it,' she said, the stock parental response to anything too difficult to deal with immediately. 'But you must promise me you won't leave school like that and run off ever again.'

'I already promised,' Stephen said, his bottom lip sticking out.

'And if he comes to the school to see you, you aren't to go with him.'

'Why would he do that?' he asked, clearly puzzled.

'I don't know. But you mustn't go anywhere with anyone unless I know about it, OK?'

'OK. Am I in trouble at school?'

She shook her head. 'No. You're not in trouble, darling. We were just all worried about you.' And they won't let you out of sight ever again if I have anything to do with it, because I'd die if anything happened to you, but only after I'd killed anyone who would harm so much as a single hair on your precious head—

'Mummy, what did Michael do wrong? Why are you so frightened of him? I thought you were friends.'

Oh, Lord. The perception of the child.

'He lied to me,' she said.

'But he wouldn't hurt me,' he said again.

What kind of a monster do you think I am?

'I'll talk to him,' she promised.

'Today?'

'Maybe. Do you think Ed's mum would let you stay again tonight, so I can go and talk to him?'

He nodded. 'She said I could stay there till our house was mended, if I like.'

'I'll do it tonight then.'

If I can find the courage…

'Michael?'

He opened his eyes and stared at her, wondering if she was really there or if he'd conjured her up out of his desperate imagination.

No. She was real—and she looked scared to death. He sat up slowly, dried his hands and reached for the remote, turning off the music that was threatening to blow the barn apart.

The silence was shattering, broken only by the bubbling of the Jacuzzi, and right on cue even that fell silent.

'I rang the bell. I couldn't make you hear,' she said, her hands twisting together.

'Sorry. I had the music on.' Idiot. She knows you had the music on. Oh, Annie, don't look at me like that—

'I'll get out,' he said and, reaching for the towel, he stood up, turning his back so she didn't start accusing him of anything else.

He heard the sound of her indrawn breath.

The scars. Damn. He hadn't even thought of it, but no

doubt seeing them in the oblique lighting of the barn would just enhance the horror of the livid ridges and corrugated flesh. That was why he'd kept his robe on at the hotel.

He turned slowly to face her, the towel wrapped firmly round his waist. 'I'm sorry. I'm not a pretty sight.'

'That tree could have killed you,' she said, and he realised she wasn't talking about the scars at all, but about the bruises that he hadn't even looked at.

'I'm fine, Annie.'

'It could have killed all of us if it wasn't for you. I wanted to thank you.'

He shrugged into a robe, walked through into the kitchen, took a glass and filled it with iced water, drained it. 'For what?' he asked bitterly. 'Saving my son's life?'

There. It was said, and it vibrated in the air between them like some kind of emotional gauntlet. Would she have the courage to pick it up?

Annie swallowed. 'Ruth said I should listen to you—hear what you had to say. Tim said I should give you a chance. But I'm scared, Michael. Or Etienne. You see, I don't even know who you are—'

'My name's Michael Armstrong,' he said, his voice flat and expressionless. 'I'm thirty-eight, I left school at eighteen and joined the army. My mother died when I was twenty, my father a year later. I was recruited into military intelligence. My mother was French—the wine we drank the other night came from my uncle's vineyard. That's how I knew so much about wine, from staying with Antoine in the summers when I was growing up. I was raised bilingual. My godmother's name is Peggy, my godfather's Malcolm. They're the nearest thing I have to parents, and until three weeks ago, they thought I was dead. They now know I'm alive.'

She stared at him, taking it all in slowly, wondering how his poor godparents must have felt all that time. No. She knew how they'd felt. 'Do you still work for the military?'

He shook his head. 'No. I was invalided out. They gave me a new identity—a new start.'

'And you came here. Why?'

He sighed and rammed a hand through his hair, wincing when he caught the bump with his fingertips. 'I wanted to make sure you were all right. You'd told me where you were going, what you were going to do. It made it easy to find you.'

She shivered. Even then, all that time ago, he had been following her—

'Did you use me, as part of your cover? In France. Did you use me to give yourself more credibility?'

He shook his head, but his answer wasn't what she'd expected. It was far more chilling. 'No—although it wouldn't have hurt my cover at all. I kept close to you because I didn't like the way Gaultier was looking at you. I knew what the bastard was capable of, and I wanted to make sure you were safe. Falling in love with you was a complication I could have done without, though.'

She flinched at the brutal honesty of that remark, but he was obviously done with lies. He went on.

'I came to find you once I was out of hospital, and discovered you were married and you had a child. But the register of births didn't show a father's name, so I didn't think it could be Roger, or you would have put him down. And besides, you called him Stephen. Etienne is French for Stephen, and I was vain enough to imagine you might have called him after me.'

He looked away. 'I bought this barn and started converting it. It helped my mind work, helped the writing. Gave me some kind of physical outlet. And I could watch over you. I had a motorbike, and I used to ride through the market square and try and catch a glimpse of you. And then the Ancient House came up for sale, just after I sold my first book, and so I bought it with the advance, and moved Ruth in there.

'She needed somewhere to live, she'd been through hell and was still not right, but she wanted to live alone again. She'd been here with me until then, roughing it on a building site but preferring it to being vulnerable. Did she tell you what happened?'

'She said she was raped.'

He snorted. 'She had a system—when it all got too tight for comfort, when it looked as if the punters were going to get serious and she needed to get out, she'd press her pager and an officer in a car would cruise round the corner and pick her up, pretending to be a customer. Then one night the car didn't come. It was held up in traffic, some stupid shunt. He came running on foot, just in time to see her being dragged into a car.'

A muscle worked in his jaw. 'I saw the forensics. There were twelve men, at least. She nearly died. They had to do a hysterectomy to save her. She'll never have children, but I think it's a miracle she can have a relationship with a man at all. It says a lot about Tim and the kind of man he is.'

She felt her eyes fill with tears. Talk about above and beyond the call of duty. So much sacrifice. She began to get a feel for what they'd all been through, but still, she couldn't understand why he hadn't come clean as soon as he could.

She searched his face, looking for clues. For the elusive truth. 'Why didn't you tell me who you were? I mean, I know you couldn't before, but when you could? Why didn't you say something then? Why carry on the lie?'

He sighed, dragging his fingers through his hair again,

wincing again as he forgot the bruise. 'Because I wanted
to know if you could love me. Me, Michael—not Etienne,
not the father of your child, but me, the man I am now, the
real man, not the man I was pretending to be, the man you
thought you loved. And I wanted to know if I loved you
still, loved the woman you'd become. The wife, the mother,
the businesswoman. You were just a girl. You might have
changed—but you hadn't.'

His voice softened. 'You were still Annie, and I knew
the moment I spoke to you that nothing felt any different.
I still loved you. I still do. More now than ever. And I'm
sorry I blew it. I was going to tell you on Sunday night,
but the tree got in the way.'

She wasn't going to give in. Not yet, not when there
were still things she needed to have answered. She wrapped
her arms round her, hugging herself. 'You spied on me for
nine years, Michael. Do you have any idea what that makes
me feel like? To have been stalked, all that time?'

'No,' he said harshly. 'I wasn't stalking you, Annie. I
was keeping you safe. If Gaultier had come after you to
get more information on me—I'd seen the way he looked
at you. He wanted you, Annie. As long as he was alive, I
didn't think you were safe, and I couldn't watch you myself, so Ruth did it for me. To keep you safe.'

She shuddered, not wanting to think about Gaultier. 'And
Roger? You set up a meeting, deliberately, while I was out.
Why did you need to meet him?'

He looked away. 'You were married to him. He was
bringing up my son. I wanted to be sure he was kind to
you. When I came after you, I was hoping you'd still be
single, that this business with Gaultier would be cleared up
in a few months. But you were married, and there was a
baby, and months turned to years. It looked as if I might

never get a chance to be with you, but I could still keep you safe. And then Roger died.'

'And if he hadn't?'

'Then I would have come to you when Gaultier was out of the way and told you both the truth. Asked for a chance to get to know my son, to have a part in his life. I knew from Ruth that you'd told Stephen about Etienne, that he knew Roger was his stepfather. But I swear, I would have done nothing without talking to you. I don't want to harm any of you, Annie. I just want a chance to take care of you. To make you happy.'

'But you *lied* to me, you and Ruth!' she said, her tears of anguish and betrayal welling over. 'You made a fool of me, when I should have recognised you. Why? You should have trusted me—you should have known I'd love you.'

'I did trust you, but I didn't know any such thing. I knew you collected lame ducks, and I didn't want to be one of them. I just didn't want your pity.' He swallowed and turned away so she couldn't see his expression.

'I needed to know that you could still want me for myself, and not just because of some misplaced loyalty to Stephen's father or because you felt sorry for me—'

'Sorry for you? Why should I feel sorry for you? You're hugely successful, you've got vast amounts of money, you could have anyone you wanted. Why should I feel sorry for you, for God's sake?'

'Because you *didn't* recognise me. Because *I* don't recognise me. Because of this face—'

'But your face is fine,' she said, confused. 'OK, it's not your original face, but it's all right. It's just a face. What's wrong with that?'

He turned back to her, his eyes anguished. 'What's wrong? It's disfigured, that's what's wrong. It isn't me, Annie. Not only am I not called my proper name, but I don't even look like me any more. And I know you well enough to know how kind you are. I didn't want to wake up one day and find you'd married me for the wrong reasons, that it was pity in your eyes and not love. And so I lied, to give you time to fall in love with me, and it backfired. Well, Ruth warned me. She said it was stupid. She told me I'd blow it, and she was right.'

His voice cracked and he turned away abruptly. 'I can't do this any more, Annie. I've done all I can. You're safe now, both of you, that's all that really matters. Stephen's got the money, you've got this house—'

'What money?' she asked, confused. 'What house?'

'The trust fund. That legacy from a cousin who didn't exist.'

She felt her stomach drop. 'That was you? You gave Stephen nearly half a million pounds, just like that?'

'I didn't want you to have to stay with Roger if you weren't happy. I thought if you had financial independence, you could start again somewhere else. There was provision for it to be used for housing you both. And this house— it's in your name. You can do what you like with it. Just give me a few days to pack up and get out. I did it all for you anyway—I thought you'd like it, because of the barn in France you said you liked that day.'

'Up in the hills,' she said slowly. 'You remembered.'

'I remember everything about us,' he told her, turning back to face her, his eyes ravaged with pain and regret. 'Every last, incredible moment. And Cardiff. Another one for the memory banks. I shouldn't have done it. Shouldn't have made love to you, either time. But I wasn't strong enough to walk away from you, and wrong as it was, I can't regret it. France, because it gave the world our son, and Cardiff—how could I regret anything so beautiful?'

He reached out, picked up a bunch of keys, held them out to her.

'Here. The keys of your house—with my love. I'm sorry it didn't work for us. I hope you'll both be happy.'

The keys fell through her fingers, and she stared at him, searching his face and finding what she was looking for. At last.

'I did know you,' she said in wonder. 'When you came in. My heart nearly stopped. You said I looked as if I'd seen a ghost, and maybe I had, because it's all still there when I look closely. I just wasn't expecting it, because I knew you were dead, so I reasoned it away.' She stooped and picked up the keys, put them back on the side, let out her breath on a rush.

'I'm sorry,' she whispered, tears spilling down her face. 'I've been such a fool. I was just so scared. This thing's so big—it isn't every day a person like me gets tangled up in some international incident. I didn't know who to speak to, how to know if Stephen was safe. I should have known you couldn't hurt him. I'm sorry. Forgive me. I shouldn't have doubted you—not for a moment. You promised I could trust you. I should have listened to you.'

For an age he stood there staring at her, then with a ragged groan he folded her against his chest and held her tight.

'Oh, God, I thought I'd lost you,' he said unsteadily, and his lips found hers and he kissed her as if he'd die without her. Then he lifted his head and stared down into her eyes, the tears clumping on his lashes. 'Marry me,' he said. 'Please. If you want to. Let me be with you. We can live wherever you like, do whatever you want. The girls can come, too, if you like. You don't even have to marry me if you don't want to. Just say you'll be with me, all of you.'

'Even Vicky?'

He laughed, the sound music to her ears. 'Even Vicky. She's lovely. I'll even put up with the cat if I have to.'

His hands slid to her shoulders, held her away so he could search her eyes. 'Answer me, Annie, for pity's sake,' he said, his voice now shaking with emotion.

'Yes,' she said. 'Oh, yes, my darling. I'll marry you.'

'Thank God,' he said raggedly. 'Oh, thank God.' He drew her back into his arms and held her close. 'What are we going to tell Stephen?'

'The truth,' she said. 'That you were hurt, that I thought you were dead, that you've been waiting for us until it was safe. He loves you, Michael. He knew you wouldn't hurt him—and it took him to tell me.'

'We'll go now—bring him back here, where he belongs.'

'Perhaps you need to get dressed first.'

He gave a strained chuckle. 'Give me five minutes.'

'You're my father? My real father? The Frenchman?'

Michael nodded. 'Yes.' It was all he could manage. The emotion was choking him, and after shutting it all down for so long, there was a hell of a lot of it to deal with.

'But I thought you were dead?'

'So did I,' his mother said gently. 'But he wasn't. He just couldn't tell us.'

'Why?'

He drew Stephen closer. 'Because in the army there are some things that have to be secret, even from the people you love,' he explained simply.

'But you're allowed to not be secret now?'

He nodded. 'That's why I'm here.'

'Why didn't Mummy know you?'

'Because I look different. My face was hurt, and it's changed the way I look. But my eyes are still the same as yours. See.'

He took Stephen's hand, led him to the mirror in the hall. 'Can you see?'

They met each other's eyes in the glass, and Stephen nodded. 'They're the same.' And then he smiled and said, 'So—can I call you Daddy?' and Michael thought his heart would burst.

He couldn't speak. He just nodded, and then Stephen was in his arms, and Annie too, and he forgot the pain. Forgot everything except the future, and that was going to be just fine...

It was hours later, and Stephen was finally asleep, out for the count in the guest bedroom at one end of the suspended steel walkway that linked the two upper rooms at each end of the barn. Annie and Michael lay naked on the huge bed in the master bedroom at the other end, the lights on full as she traced the network of scars on his body with her fingertip. Learning him, his history, charting every single nick and graze that had ever happened to him.

Her finger hesitated over a puckered line along his ribs. 'What's this one?'

'A gunshot. I got it the year before I went to France.'

'And this?'

She drew her finger along the length of the great, curving scar that went from spine to navel around his waist. 'That was France. I had a ruptured kidney, they had to remove it.'

'And this?'

'Liver. They sorted it. It's fine now.'

She touched his face again, her fingers gentle, seeking. She touched his chin, opened his mouth, looked at his teeth, finding tiny scars in his mouth to show how the surgeons had done their miraculous work on his face. It must have hurt so much. 'You were very lucky,' she said softly.

He laughed with only a trace of bitterness. 'I didn't feel lucky at the time.'

'In the hospital, you were talking about morphine.'

He couldn't suppress the shudder. 'I got a bit hooked,' he said. 'Coming off it was hell, but it was better than the alternative.'

Her eyes filled with tears, and she kissed him gently, her lips touching every wound, every mark and nick and scratch on him, healing him inside as well as out.

'I'm so sorry. You must have been in so much pain.'

He shrugged. 'It happens. It's called collateral damage. David's death, what happened to me, what happened to Ruth—we all know it's out there. We just have to hope it doesn't get us. At least it's over now and we know it's finished.'

A shiver went over her, and she snuggled closer. 'Tell me about that night,' she said, curling into his side and resting a hand over his heart, so she could feel the deep, steady, even beat that told her he was indeed alive.

'It was stupid. Things like that so often are. Somebody told David about Ruth when he checked in to report something, and he went out of his mind. He grabbed me and dragged me to one side, and muttered something to me in English. I thought we'd got away with it, but then I realised we were getting funny looks. Our cover was blown. I told him—said we had to get out that night. We should have gone straight away, but he didn't want to arouse any more suspicion, and there was one more thing he wanted to check.

'I should have said no. I was in charge, and I should have just got us out, but it gave me time to say goodbye to you—'

He broke off, grazing her cheek gently with his thumb. 'I knew there was a good chance we'd die that night, and

I couldn't bear the thought of dying without making love to you just once before I said goodbye.'

'*Au revoir.*'

'You noticed.'

'Oh, yes. I thought of it later, realised you must have known something was going on, but I had no idea.'

He gave a humourless laugh. 'You wouldn't. If you'd known anything your life would have been in danger, too. But I couldn't resist spending those last hours with you, making love to you. And you were so incredible—so responsive, so tender. It broke my heart to leave you. I really thought I was going to die that night.'

'I knew something was going on. That's why I gave you the ring.'

'I wore it—right up until three weeks ago. I'm afraid I lost it on Sunday.'

'No. I've got it in my bag. It was in your things at the hospital. That was how I knew.'

He rolled his eyes. 'I wondered.'

'Well, that and calling yourself Armstrong. That was a bit of a give-away.'

'I can't believe I did that.'

'I can. You had a head injury. So what happened then, after you left me that night?'

'We went to town. He wanted to phone Ruth, to talk to her before we did anything else. There was a call box. We were dragged out of it, hauled down an alley and kicked to death. At least, they thought so. Something must have spooked them before they had time to finish me off, though, and I had just enough time to find my phone and dial a number that would bring in reinforcements before I passed out.'

'So someone from your team rescued you?'

He nodded. 'We were wearing tracking devices. I don't

know what was said. I just know I woke up in England in
a haze of morphine and stayed there for weeks—and that
was the good bit. Then I set about finding Ruth, to make
sure she was all right.'

'But she wasn't, was she? Tim said something about her
trying to kill herself.'

'Mmm. Guilt. Someone told her that David had been
informed about the rape, so she thought it was her fault
he'd died. It wasn't. It was mine. I should have got us
straight out, but—'

'He was a grown man. It was his own fault he blew his
cover. Don't forget he nearly got you killed, too.'

'But I was his boss.'

'I think you've paid your debt,' she said softly. She
touched his face again, her fingers trembling against the
tortured flesh. 'I'm so sorry,' she whispered, swallowing
her tears.

'I'm sorry too. Sorry I lost you, sorry that by the time
I'd found you, you were married to Roger and beyond my
reach.'

She sighed gently. 'Poor Roger. He was a lovely man,
but he was Liz's husband really till the day he died. Our
marriage was only ever in name, you know.'

He went still, then lifted his head from the pillow and
searched her eyes, his puzzled. 'In name? You didn't—?'

She shook her head, her fingers stroking him still. 'Not
once. There was never any suggestion that we should. We
had separate rooms.'

He swallowed, his Adam's apple jerking convulsively.
'If you could know how many times I've lain here and
tortured myself with an image of you with him—'

'No. There's only ever been you, in thirty years.'

He stared at her again. 'What?'

'In France—that was my first time. And Cardiff was the second.'

'And third,' he said, his voice gruff with emotion. 'Oh, Annie. I don't deserve you.'

'Oh, I think you do—but I want the truth from now on.'

'And nothing but the truth, so help me God.' His smile was wry and uncertain. 'You do trust me now, don't you?' he asked, searching her face for any last trace of doubt, but there was none.

'Yes, my darling. I trust you. I'd trust you with my life. I might as well, as it seems you've been looking after it for nine years anyway.' She pressed her lips to his jaw, over the scars. 'It's my turn now to look after you, and I intend to devote every waking minute to it—well, when I'm not working, anyway.'

'What about the tearoom?'

'What about it?'

'Do you still want to run it? You don't need to. We've got enough money, after all, you hardly need to work. You could sell it.' He hugged her gently. 'Your regulars could come here for coffee and have a swim. I wouldn't mind if it meant I had you.'

'Don't you mean my freeloaders?' she teased, and he groaned.

'OK, I'm sorry. Your friends.'

'Better. I don't know. It all depends.'

'On what?'

She lifted her face, met his eyes. 'We didn't take precautions on Sunday. If I'm pregnant—'

He felt a giant hand squeeze his heart tight. 'Is it likely?'

She shrugged. 'Maybe. And if not, we can always keep trying—if you want to?'

He felt tears well in his eyes, but he didn't care. This was Annie, and he had no secrets from her. Not now. 'Oh, yes, I want to. It ripped me apart not being there for you when you had Stephen. Missing his babyhood—' He broke off. 'I know I won't get that chance again, but another baby, that would be incredible. Maybe a sister for him—'

'Or two?'

'As many as you like. There can't be too many. I love kids. I love you. How can I be too happy?'

She laughed and snuggled closer. 'You can't—and you'll deserve every second of it. Even the dirty nappies.'

'Oh, joy,' he murmured, but he was still smiling, and he didn't think he'd ever be able to stop.